"I Was Beginning To Think You Were Trying To Avoid Me,"

Griffin said.

"Me?" Sarah diverted her gaze from his. "Why would I be avoiding you?"

He smiled. "Because you've been thinking as much as I have about the way we parted a couple of weeks ago."

She began fiddling nervously with the top button of her dress, and his gaze fixed on the movement. "I don't know what you mean," she said softly.

Griffin took a few giant steps forward to close the distance between them. Then he kissed her, long and hard and deep, pulling back only when she uttered a soft sigh of surrender.

"Now do you remember?" he asked.

Sarah's breathing was a little raspy, but she managed to whisper, "Yes, I think it's coming back to me now...."

D1402286

Dear Reader,

We here at Silhouette Desire just couldn't resist bringing you another special theme month. Have you ever wondered what it is about our heroes that enables them to win the heroines' love? Of course, these men have undeniable sex appeal, and they have charm (loads of it!), and even if they're rough around the edges, you know that, deep down, they have tender hearts.

In a way, their magnetism, their charisma, is simply indescribable. These men are . . . simply Irresistible! This month, we think we've picked six heroes who are going to knock your socks off! And when these six irresistible men meet six *very* unattainable women, passion flares, sparks fly—and *you* get hours of reading pleasure!

And what month would be complete without a terrific *Man of the Month?* Delightful Dixie Browning has created a man to remember in Stone McCloud, the hero of *Lucy and the Stone. Man of the Month* fun just keeps on coming in upcoming months, with exciting love stories by Jackie Merritt, Joan Hohl, Barbara Boswell, Annette Broadrick, Lass Small and a *second* 1994 *Man of the Month* book by Ann Major.

So don't miss a single Silhouette Desire book! And, until next month, happy reading from . . .

Lucia Macro
Senior Editor

Please address questions and book requests to:
Reader Service
U.S.: P.O. Box 1325, Buffalo, NY 14269
Canadian: P.O. Box 1050, Niagara Falls, Ont. L2E 7G7

ELIZABETH BEVARLY
A LAWLESS MAN

SILHOUETTE *Desire*®
Published by Silhouette Books
America's Publisher of Contemporary Romance

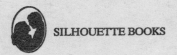

SILHOUETTE BOOKS

ISBN 0-373-05856-X

A LAWLESS MAN

ELIZABETH BEVARLY

is an honors graduate of the University of Louisville who achieved her dream of writing full-time before she even turned thirty! At heart, she is also an avid voyager who once helped navigate a friend's thirty-five-foot sailboat across the Bermuda Triangle. "I really love to travel," says this self-avowed beach bum. "To me, it's the best education a person can give to herself." Her dream is to one day have her own sailboat, a beautifully renovated older model forty-two footer, and to enjoy the freedom and tranquility seafaring can bring. Elizabeth likes to think she has a lot in common with the characters she creates, people who know that love and life go hand in hand.

For Brownie Troop No. 920.
See? I told you all I was thinking up
a story while the police lady was talking.
(Now, let your moms hang on to this book
until you all turn eighteen.)

One

The sound began as a faint whine, scarcely noticeable above the music blaring from the car stereo. Sarah Greenleaf simply tuned it out and turned the knob on the tape deck to the right, until Graham Parker was singing to her even more loudly about stupefaction. A warm wind burst through the open window on the driver's side, tossing her short, blond curls fiercely about her head. The sunny afternoon was hot and pleasant, just the way she liked her spring days, and unless she thought about what lay ahead when she reached her destination, she hadn't a care in the world.

Until the faint whine grew louder, and she glanced into her rearview mirror. Immediately she realized the whine was actually the screech of a siren—a siren attached to a police motorcycle. She also noticed that the policeman sitting atop the motorcycle was closing in on her fast.

Thinking he must be hot on the trail of some evildoer, Sarah downshifted and urged the brake pedal carefully toward the floor, edging her car to the side of the road as she slowed enough for him to pass. The policeman kept moving forward, but instead of shooting past her and off to right some wrong, he pulled alongside her car and offered her a very stern expression. Jabbing a leather-clad finger toward the right, he also mouthed the words "Pull over." Only then did she realize the evildoer he was pursuing was apparently none other than she herself.

She reacted as he requested, more out of shocked surprise than any sense of duty or submission to authority. She'd been doing nothing wrong—of that she was certain. No doubt this was some mix-up that would soon be rectified, and then she could be on her merry way. As she rolled her little Volkswagen Beetle to a halt, she glanced at her watch and frowned. She was already fifteen minutes late for lunch with Wally. Her brother was difficult enough to deal with when he'd been kept waiting. Now Officer Motorcycle Man was about to make Sarah even later, and the afternoon with Wally would be even more strained than usual as a result.

She glanced anxiously in her rearview mirror again, pushing back her overly long bangs, watching every move the policeman made. He seemed to take his time in steadying the big machine beneath him, his foot clad in a shiny black leather boot pushing down the kickstand with much familiarity. Nearly everything about the man was black, right down to the skintight jodhpurs and short-sleeved shirt that had earned the Clemente, Ohio, Police Department some strange fashion award two years in a row. As he drew nearer, she saw that his helmet, gloves, mustache and aviator-style sunglasses were black, too, the final item reflecting the sun as if two fiery orbs burned behind the lenses. Sarah swallowed with some difficulty as the policeman paused by her window, then she pushed her sunglasses to the top of her head.

"Hi," she greeted him cheerfully. "Is there a problem, Officer?"

"Turn the music down, please" was all he said in reply.

Obediently she punched the cassette from the tape player and switched it off.

"License and registration," he stated efficiently.

Even his voice was dark, she thought as she leaned across to the passenger side for her purse. When she'd extracted her driver's license from her wallet, she reached for the glove compartment to search for her registration.

"Move slowly, please," the policeman added in a no-nonsense tone of voice. "No sudden moves."

Sarah turned to gape at him. What did he think she was going to do, pull a gun on him? He must be joking. Sarah Rose Greenleaf-Markham-back-to-Greenleaf-again, den mother, room mother, PTA representative, coordinator of the annual Fulton Street bake sale and all-around normal citizen, packing a piece? Honestly, it was too funny even to consider. Without commenting, she reached for the glove compartment again and punched the metal button with her thumb. But instead of flipping open, the door remained steadfastly shut. She stabbed the button once more, to no avail.

Sarah sighed in frustration. She dearly loved her thirty-year-old Volkswagen Beetle. Unfortunately, time had not been good to the little car. She still carried fond memories of her teenage revels in the yellow Bug, and of driving it to college out of state for the first time.

But these days, the Bug was no more a bright, excited kid than she was. Both of them had left their shining youths long behind. Sarah was three years older than her car, a divorced mother of two, and her little VW had become more of a liability than a fun possession. She dreaded to think how she would stand up to a similar comparison.

Still, anything that went wrong with the Bug she could pretty much fix herself. She even knew how to rebuild the engine if times called for such an overhaul. The fact that she knew how her car worked better than she understood the workings of her own mind was what had kept her from trading it in for something new and unfamiliar. That and the fact that she just couldn't afford something new right now.

Optimistically she tried to curl her fingertips under the glove-compartment door and yank hard as she pushed the button one last time. But the effort was futile. The door remained fixed tight.

She turned back to offer the policeman a nervous smile. "It's jammed," she said unnecessarily. "This, ah, this happens a lot. Well, not a lot, actually. But sometimes." She kept her gaze level with his as she repeatedly bashed the oblong piece of metal with her doubled fist. "When it's... most... inconvenient."

The policeman did not seem to be amused. With a sigh that fell somewhere between impatience and resignation, he surveyed Sarah intently, one hand settled on an intriguingly trim hip, the other placed menacingly on the butt of his gun. It was a position she duly noted, and she couldn't help herself when she held up her hands in a gesture of surrender that was only half-joking.

"The registration is in there, I swear it," she told him. "I just can't get the stupid door open." After a moment's pause, she added hopefully, "Maybe... maybe you could give it a shot?"

"Lady, I—"

He stopped speaking as quickly as he'd started, sighed deeply again, then shook his head as if he couldn't believe what was happening to him. For the first time, Sarah noticed the name tag pinned to his shirt above his badge. Lawless, it said. She wondered if that was indeed his name, or some kind of dubious honor the department had bestowed upon him.

"Your name is Lawless?" she asked before she could stop herself, unable to halt the smile she felt forming. "A cop named Lawless?"

"Yeah," he replied wearily.

His tone assured her he had been through this before and did not intend to go through it again with her. Sarah chose not to pursue the subject and instead worried her lower lip with her teeth. Out of nowhere, she wondered what color his eyes were behind the dark glasses. Probably black, just like everything else about him, she thought. Gingerly she extended her license toward him in silence, but Officer Lawless didn't take it right away. He only continued to stare at her in that maddeningly accusatory manner.

"I'd give you the registration, too, but I can't get the glove compartment open," she reminded him.

The policeman drew in a deep breath. "Unlock the passenger-side door," he told her. She got the feeling his statement was pulled from him reluctantly.

As he made his way around the front of the car to the other side, Sarah could have sworn he was mumbling to himself. He jerked open the door opposite her, bent forward and struggled with the glove compartment in much the same way she had done only moments earlier.

"See?" she said, not quite able to keep herself from gloating. "I told you so."

Officer Lawless glared at her. At least, Sarah thought he was glaring. It was hard to tell with those dark glasses hiding his eyes. No matter what, though, she could sense without a doubt that he was getting pretty steamed.

He folded himself into the car seat beside her, and suddenly the little vehicle seemed microscopic. She hadn't really noticed how big the policeman was when he was standing outside her window. Everyone seemed tall when one was sitting—especially when one was sitting in a Volkswagen Beetle. But now Officer Lawless was sitting, too, and he still seemed to tower over her. In the close confines of the car, with the sun beating through the windshield, she could feel the heat radiating off his body in enticing waves. His black leather boot creaked when he pulled one foot inside the car for leverage, and she noted almost absently the silver handcuffs shoved beneath his belt.

An odd thrill of excitement wound through her as she envisioned herself sharing an activity with Officer Lawless for which those handcuffs were never intended.

Sarah marveled at the waywardness of her thoughts, feeling her skin heat all over as she tried unsuccessfully to push the graphic image away. Clearly she had been too long without the attentions of a man, she thought. Or maybe she just wasn't getting enough calcium. She'd been reading about that lately.

As she pondered the curiousness of her uncharacteristic fantasy, Officer Lawless gave the glove compartment one final thump with the heel of his hand, and the door sprang open. Her delight with his success was quickly compounded by her embarrassment when the entire contents spilled out into his lap. Amid the occasional necessities like maps, flashlight and tissues, there fell a seemingly endless cascade of ketchup and soy sauce packets, abstract Lego creations, socks, GI Joe action figures, lipsticks and mismatched earrings.

Sarah grabbed up one of those last items. "Well, would you look at that?" she asked no one in particular. "I've been searching all over for this." She clipped the earring into place and shook her hair back so that she could inspect the effect in the rearview mirror. "What else is in there?" she added as she spared a glance at Officer Lawless's lap.

Why did no one carry gloves in their glove compartment? she wondered idly as her gaze picked absently through the assortment of stuff that had spilled. Her eyes finally settled on a perfectly square, foil-wrapped packet that had fallen into a *very* significant place on the policeman. A condom? she gasped inwardly. Heavens, where had that come from? It must be one of Michael's. But she and Michael had been divorced for more than three years. Just how long had it been since she had cleaned out the glove compartment?

Sarah started to reach for the item in question, until Officer Lawless seemed to realize where she was headed and intercepted her hand before it made contact with its target. He gripped her wrist fiercely with one hand sheathed in black leather and scooped up the condom with the other. Lifting it to eye level, he turned his attention to her more fully, then cocked his left eyebrow with much interest.

"I—it must belong to my husband," she stammered. "I mean . . . he's not my husband, but . . ."

Officer Lawless's right eyebrow joined his left.

"I mean . . . uh . . ." Oh, dear. Just what did she mean?

"Never mind," Officer Lawless said. He dropped the condom into the glove compartment and began to gather up the remaining contents and return them to their original resting place.

Griffin Lawless couldn't believe this was happening to him. He picked gingerly through the assortment of odds and ends on his lap as if they were radioactive, all the while wondering what kind of person would drive around with so many unnecessary accoutrements. He stared at the woman beside him as he tried to figure her out. He had noticed the moment he'd sat down in her car that she smelled wonderful, a strangely floral fragrance he found incongruent with her ragged jeans and T-shirt. Her hair was a riot of blond curls falling over her forehead and spilling down around her ears, and her brown eyes were as dark and guileless as a beagle puppy's.

Absently he realized his fingers still encircled her wrist, and he glanced down at her hand. Strong-looking, raw-boned, with nails bitten down to the quick and Band-Aids on her index and ring fingers. Probably because she had hangnails, he thought. He released her then, and watched as she anxiously brushed her hair behind one ear. Still wearing the one long, dangling earring, she looked, for some reason, like an abandoned street waif.

Griffin frowned. He did not care for women like her—women who had no concern for their appearance, no control over their nerves. This was just what he needed after the kind of day he'd already had. One more bizarre encounter in a string of bizarre encounters. The condom had been an interesting touch, though. She didn't seem the type to carry something like that around. And who was this guy who was, then wasn't, her husband?

He was still wondering about that when he realized the woman beside him had started helping to collect her things and put them back in the glove compartment. Nimble fingers skimmed over his thighs in a way that made Griffin hold his breath and swallow hard. She seemed to have no idea of the possible implication behind her activity. When her fingers began to travel a little higher than they should, he jumped up and struggled to get out of the car, spilling the few items left in his lap onto the floor and bumping his head severely. Fortunately he was still wearing his helmet. That didn't help him, however, when he slammed the car door shut and caught the end of his finger in the process.

"Ow, dammit," he cursed as he cradled his injured hand in his good one.

He made his way back around the front of the car, eyeing the woman in the driver's seat suspiciously. Some college kid, he guessed. She gazed back at him steadily, but looked plenty worried. Which of course was fine with him. Why should she be comfortable when he was feeling so agitated himself?

When Griffin stood beside the driver's-side window once again, he squared his shoulders resolutely, flexed the fingers of his injured hand and stated, as if the past several minutes had never occurred, "License and registration."

The woman beside him smiled nervously again, then reached across the seat and began to pick through the glove compartment. He watched her intently, assuring himself his interest was only idle curiosity. The way her yellow T-shirt strained against her back let him know she wasn't wearing a brassiere, and his eyes lingered at the waistband of her faded blue jeans before dipping lower to inspect the slight flare of her hips. She was a little slim by his standards, but not too bad. He was still considering that fact when she turned back around and caught him ogling her, and her triumphant expression at having found her registration quickly turned sour.

"See anything you like?" she snapped.

Griffin reached for the registration without comment, then extended his hand for her license, as well. The woman slapped it into his palm silently, her eyes flashing with a combative fire.

After he'd scanned both documents, he asked, "Ms. Greenleaf, do you realize how fast you were going back there?"

"About thirty-five?" she asked hopefully.

"Try forty-five."

She shook her head vehemently. "There's no way I could have been going that fast. I—"

"Forty-five in a school zone," he clarified further.

"A school zone? That's not a school zone. Not now, anyway. Not at noon."

"Yes, ma'am, at noon. A lot of those kids go home for lunch."

Well, this was the first Sarah had ever heard of that. Of course, she didn't normally drive this way when she was meeting her brother for lunch, but since she'd been running so late, she had opted to try for a shortcut. She was about to explain that to him, but Officer Lawless had disappeared with her identification, and she realized belatedly he had returned to his motorcycle, presumably to run a check on her. The thought that he could be so suspicious of her character insulted Sarah as much as anything else he'd said, and she fumed silently as she awaited his return.

"Officer, I can explain," she said when the policeman stood beside her window once again.

He said nothing in reply, but cocked his left brow in that curious way again. The gesture, along with his silence, indicated to Sarah that he was at least willing to listen.

"I was running late for an appointment," she began.

ture, she couldn't afford a seventy-five-dollar speeding ticket.

"Seventy-five dollars?" she cried when she saw the total.

Officer Lawless remained his usual stoic self as he nodded. Sarah felt moisture forming under her arms and between her breasts, noted that he still seemed as cool and collected as ever, and wondered what it would take to make him break into a really good sweat.

"Yes, ma'am. Seventy-five dollars is the fine for going twenty miles an hour over the speed limit in a school zone."

"But I told you I wasn't going forty-five."

"And I told you that you were."

Sarah narrowed her eyes at him fitfully. This was not going well—not well at all. She'd always had a problem with authority figures, ever since she'd been sent to the principal's office in first grade for throwing spitballs at Bobby Burgess, even though Bobby had started it. That was probably what had gone wrong with her marriage. Not that she threw spitballs, of course, but that her ex-husband had always pulled an authoritative routine that had nearly driven her mad.

"Well, I can't afford seventy-five dollars," she told Officer Lawless, handing back the ticket and pen without signing, as if in refusing her signature, she would no longer be responsible for her transgression. "Sorry."

But instead of taking the ticket back, Officer Lawless only continued to stare at her. "You could always opt for traffic school," he suggested.

"Traffic school," Sarah repeated. "I've heard about that. Isn't that where they put you in a dark room and show you that gory, horrible film about reckless driving, with children getting decapitated and animals being run down mercilessly until there's nothing left of them but an oily spot on the road?" She thought for a moment. "Or do the animals get decapitated and the children get run down...? Well, anyway, thanks, but I can see that stuff at my local cinema at my own convenience. I don't think I want to go to traffic school."

She noticed a slight twitch in Officer Lawless's jaw before he set his teeth more completely on edge. He bent forward until his face filled the driver's-side window, and suddenly Sarah wondered what madness had overcome her to make her spar with him in the first place.

"Well, then, Ms. Greenleaf," he said in a low, level, utterly dangerous voice, "in that case, I could take you downtown in handcuffs right now and tell everyone you resisted arrest."

Sarah opened her mouth to argue, decided quickly that such a reaction would get her nowhere—except maybe booked into a suite at the Hoosegow Hilton—then scrawled her name illegibly on the ticket beside the place where Officer Lawless had so thoughtfully provided her with an X to mark the spot.

"I'm going to argue with the judge over this, you know," she assured her tormentor as she handed the ticket book back to him.

Officer Lawless smiled for the first time as he tore off her copy of the ticket, and Sarah became furious with herself that she found his smile so appealing.

"Well, then, Ms. Greenleaf," he said as he dropped the ticket through the window and into her lap, "I look forward to seeing you in court. Have a nice day."

Only after he'd turned and walked casually back to his motorcycle did Sarah bravely whisper the word *Pig.* She watched in her rearview mirror as he straddled his big motorcycle and shoved back the kickstand with his boot, throttled the machine to a rousing roar, then sped off past her, spewing gravel in his wake.

Sarah wadded up the ticket and stuffed it into her purse, grumbling about fascism and police states, ill-tempered brothers and men in general, then urged her own little car to sputtering life. She was not having a nice day. Worse than that, she knew it wasn't going to get better anytime soon.

She could tell immediately that she'd lost him with that. No doubt he'd been hoping for something really creative and juicy—that she was being followed by body-snatching pea pods from outer space, or was on her way to meet Elvis, who had been spotted working as a pastry chef at the local thrift bakery. Officer Lawless dropped his gaze back to her license and registration, then pulled a ticket book from nowhere and began to write.

"No, really," she said, trying again. "I was supposed to meet my brother, Wally, twenty minutes ago, and he hates to be kept waiting. Actually, he's kind of a jerk, but it's only because he's so insecure. If I told him that, though, he'd go through the roof. Besides, I'm always late when I'm supposed to meet my brother. I suppose that's psychologically significant, but, then, how many brothers and sisters get along, you know? Of course, Wally would probably blame my always being late on the fact that my parents divorced sixteen years ago, and then he'd ask me if I ever called that analyst he recommended, and I just don't want to get into that with him again...."

Sarah's voice trailed off when she realized how hysterical she was beginning to sound. Honestly, the moment she got nervous, she always started running off at the mouth like nobody's business. When she saw that Officer Lawless was no longer listening, she tried a new tack.

"Would you believe I was being followed by aliens?"

His pen paused about halfway down the page on which he was writing, but he didn't look up.

"Or that I was on my way to meet ... ? Oh, never mind."

The pen began to scratch back and forth again.

Sarah sighed. This was just what she needed. She couldn't afford to be late meeting Wally. She couldn't afford another one of his long-winded monologues about how badly she'd screwed up her life since her divorce. Most of all, she decided further when Officer Lawless stuck the ticket book and pen under her nose with a silent demand for her signa-

* * *

Late that Friday afternoon found Griffin Lawless sitting on a bench in the locker room at the police station, staring thoughtfully into his locker. Man, it had been a bitch of a week. Vaguely he noted the calendar taped to the inside of the scarred metal door, a collection of dates that seemed meaningless now somehow. He had a dentist's appointment next Thursday...a date with that new redhead in homicide tomorrow evening...that Cub Scout career-night thing on Monday.

His eyes wandered over all these appointments until his gaze fell on one date marked in bright-red ink, circled five times for effect. His great-grandfather's ninety-fifth birthday would have been next Friday. It was the day Griffin was to have met the old man for the first time. Now he never would. Because his great-grandfather had never made it back to the States from wintering in New Zealand, and now the old man's body was resting quietly at sea.

An attorney had telephoned last week with the news of Harold Mercer's death, and to confirm that Griffin Lawless was the sole living relative and heir to the Mercer holdings. It was strange to think now, that the family name so famous for wealth and refinement around the suburban community of Clemente, Ohio, would turn out to be Griffin's own. He'd grown up knowing of the Mercers as everyone else in Clemente had, as the town's richest, most illustrious citizens. Who would have ever guessed that he was one of them?

He wadded up the black uniform shirt in his hands and stuffed it unceremoniously into a wrinkled duffel bag. The boots came off next, falling to the floor with a slow *thump... thump,* then Griffin pushed himself up from the bench with a ragged groan to remove his black jodhpurs. He rotated his left shoulder to alleviate the stiffness still present from his wound, then headed for the showers.

He leaned into the swirls of steam that rose around him, letting the moist heat rush into his pores and sore muscles, easing the tension that resulted from a combination of many things—the remnants of pain from a gunshot wound that was scarcely two months healed; the frustration of finding a family he never knew he had only to lose it again so quickly; the odd, sudden realization that life was passing so quickly, too quickly for him to stop and enjoy it for a while...

The lingering fragrance of flowers he couldn't quite dispel from his memory, a fragrance that brought with it the reminder of coffee brown eyes full of spirit, and blond curls that had seemed to beg him to touch.

Griffin pushed the memory away. He'd *ticketed* the woman, for God's sake, he reminded himself. Even if there was some obscure chance he might run into Ms. Sarah Greenleaf again, she wasn't likely to be receptive to any romantic overtures on his part. Still, he couldn't help but smile as he recalled the expression on her face when that condom had come tumbling out of the glove compartment along with a number of other personal belongings. He couldn't remember the last time he'd seen a human being blush with embarrassment. There weren't many people left who felt such a thing anymore.

"Griffin? You in here?"

He recognized the voice of his friend and co-worker Mitchell Stonestreet and called out, "In here, Stony."

Stony materialized through the rolling white fog, dressed in his nondescript plainclothes detective wear, his white-blond hair scarcely visible amid all the steam. His impenetrable black eyes were as piercing as ever, though, and Griffin marveled at the way they made an otherwise innocent-looking man seem utterly menacing.

"Got good news for you, pal," Stony said, holding up a white, legal-size envelope. "Captain Pierce sent me down with this for you. Your orders came through. They're bumping you upstairs. Fraud squad. Although why you'd want to hang out with us bunco guys is beyond me. You could have taken homicide or vice. What's wrong with those? Not enough man for them?"

Still naked and dripping wet—very comfortable with his masculinity, thank you very much—Griffin strode toward his friend and took the proffered envelope, running damp fingers under the flap. The paper he withdrew was engraved with the Clemente, Ohio, P.D. letterhead and quickly grew limp in the humid air. Nonetheless, the words it contained were precisely the ones he wanted to read, and he smiled.

"Homicide's a bit too grim for my tastes," he said. "And those vice guys are lunatics. But fraud... Now that's what I call a good time. Besides, Stony, I miss seeing your ugly mug every day now that you're gone from the cycle unit. Anyway, I put in for a transfer out of uniform almost two months ago. It's about damned time this came through."

He thrust the letter and envelope back toward his friend, then returned to the shower head to rinse the remnants of soap from his body. When he was through, Stony tossed him a towel, and Griffin knotted it carelessly about his waist.

"There weren't any openings until now," Stony told him. "You're replacing Tommy Gundersen. His wife got some big promotion, and they're moving west." He smiled as he added, "You and me, Griff, we'll be partners again."

"Just like old times. I hope the department knows what they're doing."

Stony chuckled. "They want you to report for duty two weeks from Monday," he said as he followed Griffin back into the locker room. "Think you can stay out of trouble on your bike until then?"

Griffin nodded impatiently. "Yeah, yeah. I'll do my best."

"No more trying to shoot it out with the bad guys one-on-one?"

Griffin scowled as he rubbed unconsciously at his shoulder again. The skin was still pink, puckered and raw-looking on both his chest and back where the entry and exit wounds had healed. "No worries there. I hope I never have to look down the barrel of a gun again. Why do you think I put in for a transfer? Uniform duty is getting too dangerous."

Stony looked at his friend doubtfully. "Too dangerous? Did I hear you correctly? This from a man who vacations in the desert just so he can go night biking without a headlight?"

Griffin smiled grimly. "Nobody shoots at me in the desert. Too many things can happen out on the streets. I want to live long enough to enjoy my retirement."

He held up a hand when Stony appeared ready to object. He knew what his friend was going to say. What was the point of retiring when he had nothing to retire to? Unfortunately Griffin couldn't quite contradict that line of thinking. Both his parents were dead, and he had no other family. Not anymore, anyway, he amended reluctantly, recalling his great-grandfather's death. He was a thirty-seven-year-old man who had very little to show for his time on Earth and no big plans in the making. Why start thinking about the future now?

Griffin tucked his black T-shirt into well-worn jeans, shoved his feet into low-heeled boots and threw his duffel bag over one shoulder before allowing himself to form an answer to his question. And the answer that finally came wasn't one that sat well with him. He was starting to think about the future now because, for some reason, lately he'd been able to think of little else.

"You got plans tonight?" he asked his friend as he collected his nondepartment-issue motorcycle helmet from the top shelf of his locker.

Stony shook his head. "Elaine's not speaking to me this weekend."

Griffin made a face. "Again? What did you do this time?"

Stony sighed with much confusion. "I have no idea."

Griffin smiled as he slammed his locker door shut. "The usual, then, huh? Want to grab a bite?"

"Sure. Why not?"

The two men chatted as Stony gathered his things, then they filed out of the locker room and into the balmy spring evening.

"You know," Stony began as they paused beside Griffin's sleek, dark Harley Davidson, "maybe you can help me figure out the feminine mystique. You've had more than your share of experience coping with it."

"Yeah, 'coping' is the appropriate word, too." Griffin donned his helmet and straddled the big machine. "And believe me, I don't understand women any better than you do. So, meet you at Delgado's?"

Stony nodded. "Whoever gets there first buys the first round."

Griffin nodded back, then slammed his foot down on the pedal, bringing the bike to roaring life. For some reason, the motion reminded him of the woman he'd encountered earlier in the afternoon, the one who had glared at him from her rearview mirror and silently mouthed the word *Pig*. He smiled when he recalled that. She probably didn't realize he'd been able to see the comment she'd made. He wondered what she would have done if he'd returned to her car, yanked her out for arrest and given her a thorough body search.

Griffin's smile broadened. She probably would have pressed charges of police brutality and sexual harassment and landed his butt in the can. Still, he thought further, remembering the smooth expanse of back beneath her yellow T-shirt, a few years in the pokey might be worth it.

Chuckling to himself, Griffin Lawless slipped his sunglasses on, urged the throttle forward and sped away. Ms. Sarah Greenleaf would just be a memory from now on, and there was no reason for him to dwell on her anymore.

Still, he thought, she had smelled wonderful. And he didn't think he'd seen anyone with eyes that brown before. He wondered if her hair was as soft as it had looked. . . .

Two

"**S**o how was lunch with your brother on Friday?"

Sarah looked up from icing a lopsided chocolate cake to throw her friend Elaine Bingham a grim look. "Same as always. Wally just can't understand why I'm not as wildly ambitious and successful as he is. He's convinced I ruined my life when I divorced Michael."

"Well, tell him to lay off," Elaine said. "Just because he's a contractor doesn't mean he can run everything, especially your life."

Sarah nodded her agreement, wishing it were that simple. "All in all, though, I guess lunch was no worse than usual. Certainly no worse than what I experienced on the way."

Three days had passed since she had signed her name to a speeding ticket she was still certain she didn't deserve, but the passage of time had done nothing to improve a dark mood that had followed Sarah all weekend. Every time she remembered Officer Lawless in all his black glory, her back went up like a startled cat's. She didn't know why he continued to raise her hackles so long after the fact, or why she couldn't stop thinking about him, and her confusion at her behavior only enhanced the tension she felt. Now as she prepared for her house to be invaded by fifteen little Cub Scouts, she could only shake her head in wonder at her odd reaction.

"What happened before lunch?" Elaine asked from the dining room, where she was setting out paper cups and plates.

Sarah bit her lip as she tried to even out a big lump at the center of the cake. She never had been much of a cook. She was an even worse baker. "I got a speeding ticket," she said.

Elaine's expression was incredulous when she returned to the tiny kitchen from the dining room. At one time, Sarah had thought her kitchen huge. Of course, that was back when she and Michael had moved into the four-bedroom Cape Cod from a two-room apartment with a kitchen the size of a closet. Nowadays, amid all the clutter, even painting every visible surface in her kitchen white had done little to create an impression of size. And with Elaine looming in the doorway, Sarah felt the space grow even smaller.

"*You* got a speeding ticket?" her friend asked. "In that dinky car of yours? That thing doesn't go faster than ten or fifteen miles an hour, does it?"

"Very funny," Sarah said, swiping a finger across her cheek. "I don't want to talk about it."

Elaine shrugged and went back to her task. "Okay, fine. By the way, although it's really too late to be asking, you did get your four guys lined up for tonight, didn't you?"

"Yes, I got my four guys lined up for tonight," Sarah replied obediently. "And I think I did pretty well. I have an accountant, a claims adjuster, a computer programmer and a mortician."

Elaine came back into the kitchen and wrinkled her nose. "Sarah, we're having career day for a den of Cub Scouts, for

God's sake. What are those guys going to talk about with a bunch of little kids?''

Sarah lifted her chin defiantly. ''They all have perfectly lucrative jobs. Jobs that will definitely be in demand in the future, I might add.''

She couldn't help but feel a little defensive. She thought she'd done pretty well, considering the fact that she didn't know that many men to begin with. And it hadn't been easy to get these guys lined up for the meeting tonight. She was going to have to go out with two of them. ''What kind of guys did you get?'' she asked Elaine.

The other woman beamed, shook back her long, dark hair and smoothed a graceful hand over the widow's peak that Sarah so envied. ''I got an air-force fighter pilot, a baseball player—from Cincinnati, no less—a fireman and a cop.''

''A cop?'' Sarah sneered.

Elaine laughed. ''Well, if I'd known you were going to have a run-in with the law...''

''Ha, ha.''

''Anyway, Jonah is really looking forward to tonight, and I'm sure the other boys are, too.''

Sarah smiled, her defensiveness fading as she thought of her own sons. ''Yeah, Jack and Sam can't wait to see what we have planned. How on earth did you manage to draw guys from such glamorous fields? I mean, come on, Elaine, a baseball player? A Cincinnati Red?''

Elaine threw her a self-satisfied smile. ''Oh, I just called a few numbers in my little black book.''

Sarah shook her head. ''You and that little black book. I'm going to have to sneak a peek inside one of these days.''

''Hey, I've offered to set you up,'' her friend reminded her. ''Remember? There was that guy from the circus who was dying to meet you.''

''The human cannonball? No, thanks. Life with Michael was explosive enough. I want some nice, sedate, normal guy. No adventurous types.''

"Mm-hmm," Elaine remarked. "Like an accountant, maybe? Or a claims adjuster? Or a mortician?"

Sarah nodded. "Yeah, maybe. What's so terrible about being involved with a quiet man?"

"Nothing—if you don't mind being bored to death," Elaine rejoined.

"I refuse to get into this with you," Sarah said as she surrendered to the cake. It would just have to remain lopsided. "You're a woman who thinks bungee jumping is a passive sport."

"Well, it is."

Sarah couldn't help but laugh. In many ways, the two women were very different people. Elaine was tall and well rounded in all the places women were supposed to be, her black hair spilling in a straight cascade to the middle of her back, streaked with silver as if touched by a fairy's paintbrush. Her gray eyes reflected an adventurousness and passion for life that Sarah wasn't quite sure she could claim herself, as much as she might like to.

Sarah Greenleaf and Elaine Bingham had become fast friends nearly two years ago when they'd met as room mothers for their children's class. Back then, Elaine had been enrolling her son, Jonah, in the same first-grade class as Sarah's twins. Six months ago, about the same time the two women had bought an antique business together, the three boys had joined the same Cub Scout den. When asked if they'd be interested in sharing den mother duties, Sarah and Elaine had resoundingly replied yes. Nowadays, the three boys together were more like brothers than close friends, having forged a bond as immediate and as strong as the two women's had become.

Like Sarah, Elaine was also divorced, and in addition to sharing the business and the Scouting duties, the two mothers also found themselves frequently trading off babysitting and dinner patrol, thus allowing themselves the occasional free time where they might not have it at all otherwise. All in all, their friendship had become as efficient a working system as their antique business was gradually becoming.

"Oh, gosh," Elaine said suddenly as she opened the freezer door to retrieve the ice trays. "I almost forgot to tell you."

Sarah put a cover over the offending chocolate cake so she wouldn't have to look at it until later, then brushed her hands off on her shirttail. "What?"

The other woman's smile was huge. "We have an appraisal job. One of the guys who's coming tonight—the cop—recently inherited his great-grandfather's house here in Clemente, along with everything in it, and he wants us to catalogue and appraise the collection."

"Us?" Sarah asked, unable to mask her surprise.

Elaine made a face. "Of course us. Why not us?"

It was a fair question, Sarah thought. "Well, because our shop just opened last year, that's why. We still don't have all the bugs worked out of the system. Let's face it, Harper's Antiques has been a Clemente fixture for decades. They usually get all the good jobs. Why would this guy hire us?"

Elaine's eyes sparkled. "Maybe because I quoted him a price that's half what Harper's charges for an appraisal."

"Ah. Good reason."

"Plus," she added a little reluctantly, "he's a good friend of Stony's, so it's kind of a personal favor."

Sarah narrowed her eyes at her friend. "I thought you and Stony were on the outs right now." She'd only met the man in question once, but he seemed nice enough. Still, he and Elaine seemed to have their share of tiffs.

Elaine shrugged. "Outs, ins, ups, downs... Everyday brings something different. But getting the appraisal isn't the best part," she said, rushing on before Sarah could comment further.

She smiled, her friend's good humor infectious. "What's the best part?"

"Wait until you hear what house the guy inherited."

"What house?"

"The old Mercer place."

Sarah's eyes widened as she whistled low. "Wow. I'd give my eyeteeth to get a load of that old mansion up close."

The Mercer place had lain vacant for years, but Sarah remembered that when she was a child growing up in Clemente, it had been occupied by a woman named Meredith Mercer, the unmarried daughter of Judge Harold Mercer, retired. The judge had spent most of his time in the Canary Islands or someplace, and when his daughter had died, single and childless, he'd simply closed up the house and it had sat dormant and unoccupied for years.

Sarah had never really given much thought to the place, except on those rare occasions when she drove by and gazed at it longingly, wondering what treasures were hidden beyond the front door. She supposed she had assumed it was tied up in probate somehow, and that someday the old house would either change hands or be torn down. Now it appeared as if the former would be the case. Apparently Judge Mercer had been the father of more than one child. And now it looked as if Sarah's dream of inspecting the Mercer treasures might just become a reality.

"Well, it seems you're going to have the opportunity to look inside without risking dental trauma," Elaine said, voicing Sarah's thoughts out loud, "because the guy who inherited the place signed a contract with us this afternoon."

"Just like that?"

Elaine nodded, her smile reflecting her utter delight. "Just like that."

Before Sarah could ponder her friend's assertion further, the back door slammed open, and in ran three streaks of blue, laughing and shrieking as they sped by in a hurried blur. As quickly as the tumult had erupted it disappeared, and the two women could only shake their heads in wonder as they stared in the direction into which the chaos had fled.

Sarah was the one who broke the silence. "If we could harness that energy, we could heat the entire northeastern United States for a hundred winters to come."

The three boys reappeared then, Jonah a mirror image of his mother with his black hair and silver gray eyes. Jack and Sam, on the other hand looked little like brothers, let alone twins. Jack was a repeat of his father, with unruly brown curls and eyes the color of amber, while Sam resembled Sarah with his pale blond hair and dark brown eyes.

"Mrs. Stevens just pulled up with Mark and Devon," Jack announced.

"When does the pilot get here?" Jonah demanded.

"Is the cop going to bring his gun?" Sam wanted to know.

Good heavens, Sarah thought. If Nellie Stevens was already here, the other boys would be right behind. Belatedly she realized she wasn't even close to finished with all she had to do before the meeting's commencement. She glanced over at her friend for help, but only sighed with frustration. Elaine looked professional and organized in her Scouting blues, but Sarah hadn't even changed her clothes yet, and her blues were of the more casual variety—well worn and ragged jeans coupled with an equally bedraggled and much oversize chambray shirt, now generously spotted with chocolate.

"Elaine? Can you handle these guys while I go change?"

"Sure," her friend told her.

As Sarah fled down the hall, she heard the other woman tell Sam, "Yes, the cop will bring his gun. All the men coming tonight are going to wear what they would normally wear to work, so that you boys can get a well-rounded view of their professions."

The doorbell buzzed at the same time the back door rattled with another entry, and since Sarah was passing the living room, she automatically went to answer the door. Her first thought when she saw Officer Lawless standing on her front porch was that he had come to take her downtown and book her for some heinous crime like illegal use of a spatula or trying to pass off bad cakes as culinary creations. Then her gaze fixed with those same dark glasses that had so frustrated her attempts to gauge his reactions Friday, and she wondered once again what color his eyes were.

He was dressed exactly as he had been three days earlier, all black and leather. But now as Sarah stood face-to-face with the man, she noticed a few more things about him that she hadn't noticed before. With his helmet off, she realized his hair was short and razor straight, a realization that surprised her for some reason. Somehow he seemed the type to prefer long hair. Maybe short hair was a department rule. She also hadn't noticed Friday the way the muscles of his upper arms strained against the short sleeves of his shirt, or the dark hair that peeked up out of his open collar below the hollow of his throat. A few strands of silver mingled with the black of his mustache, and there was a scar on his chin that was too big to have resulted from a shaving accident. Somehow she was sure he had won the decoration in a fight, and such a certainty only made him seem that much more dangerous.

"Officer Lawless," she said before she could stop herself. "Was there something else I didn't do Friday that you forgot to cite me for?"

Instead of answering right away, Griffin took a single step backward and glanced up at the numbers above the front door. He frowned. Yeah, this was the right house all right. Dammit.

This was just what he needed. Another run-in with the intriguing, infuriating blonde who had haunted his thoughts all weekend. How the hell had he managed to end up here? He was doing this favor for a friend of Stony's because Stony had been assigned to duty tonight. And Stony's friend's name hadn't been Ms. Sarah Greenleaf. Griffin would have recognized that in an instant—and fled screaming in the other direction. So what was Sarah Greenleaf doing here?

She was every bit as enticing as he remembered, perhaps even more so when he considered what appeared to be a big glob of chocolate smeared across one cheek and more chocolate staining a good portion of her man-size shirt. She didn't look like the kind of den mother he'd had when he'd been a Cub Scout himself too many years ago to remember. Scouting had sure come a long way in three decades.

"Officer Lawless?" she asked him again. Only then did he realize he had yet to offer her some kind of greeting.

Before he could stop himself, Griffin reached out a hand and wiped the glob of chocolate off her cheek with his thumb, then pressed his thumb against his lips to suck the icing into his mouth. Her eyes widened in surprise at the intimate gesture, and he smiled.

"Could use a little more sugar and a little less salt," he said as he moved past her and into the house.

"Are you talking about the icing or about me?" he heard her ask from behind him.

Griffin spun around to meet her gaze levelly with his. "Oh, the icing is fine," he said without hesitation.

He could tell she was about to retaliate with something he was sure to find interesting, so he whipped off his sunglasses in order to get a clearer view of her pique. When he did so, her expression changed dramatically, and the mouth that had opened to voice a protest quickly snapped shut in concentration.

"Is there something wrong, Ms. Greenleaf?" he asked.

She shook her head slowly, but remained silent, staring at him in fascination, as if he'd just grown another head.

"What is it?" he insisted.

She took a tentative step forward, lifting a hand almost absently toward him. "Your eyes," she said softly as she came to a halt a few inches in front of him. "They're so..."

Her comment was, to say the least, the last thing he had expected to hear. Still, he encouraged her. "So...?"

She sighed, a sound that was restless and full of longing. "Blue," she replied quietly. "Your eyes are blue. For some reason, I thought they'd be dark, but they're not. They're..."

Her voice trailed off then, and Griffin was left wondering what else she had intended to say.

He felt an involuntary shudder wind through his body at the way Sarah Greenleaf was looking at him. For just the briefest of moments, her expression was completely open, utterly free of any ill will or pretense. And for that one stark moment, he saw in her eyes an absolute hunger like nothing he'd ever seen before. Her reaction made him feel more than a little uneasy, because he realized he was responding to her in exactly the same way. Sarah Greenleaf made him feel hungry, too. Hungry for something he couldn't quite identify, hungry for some unnameable something that he didn't until that moment realize he needed desperately in order to survive.

And then the moment was gone. Sarah returned to her earlier wariness, taking a step away from him again to close the front door.

"Excuse me," she said hastily, "I have to go change."

And as quickly as she had come into his life again, she was gone. Griffin felt strangely out of place in her home, noting his surroundings absently. The house looked like any number of other middle-class suburban homes he'd been inside in his line of work. The furnishings were big, boxy and functional, with a few personal touches in the form of plants, photographs and scattered toys. He should have realized right off that Ms. Greenleaf was married with children. Hadn't she mentioned a husband on Friday? He couldn't quite remember now. At any rate, a man would have to be crazy to come across her and let her get away.

Yet if that was the case, why had she thrown him such a longing look only a moment ago? Griffin wondered. Could it be that Mr. Greenleaf wasn't exactly adept at meeting all his wife's needs? Better yet, he wondered further, maybe her old man had taken a powder somewhere along the line.

"Whoa, who're you?"

The small voice came from behind Griffin, and he spun around to find five young boys staring at him in awe. He smiled. He knew what kind of imposing figure he appeared in uniform. Hell, being imposing had become one of his most effective weapons over the years. And knowing that adults reacted with some degree of fear, he could only imagine what a little kid might think of him. He didn't want to frighten a child, naturally, but he didn't mind if one was impressed. Too bad he'd been utterly ineffective in impressing the elusive Sarah Greenleaf to the same degree. Although, he thought further with a smile, maybe he wouldn't mind frightening her just a little. At least as much as she frightened him.

"I'm Officer Griffin Lawless," he introduced himself. "Clemente P.D. Motorcycle unit."

The tallest of the boys strode confidently forward, hand outstretched. "I'm Jack Markham. This is my little brother, Sam."

"I am not your little brother—I'm as old as you," Sam said quickly, stepping forward with considerably less aplomb than his brother.

"Nuh-uh, you are not," Jack contradicted him. "I came fifteen minutes before you. Mom said so. I'm oldest."

"Are not."

"Are, too."

"Are not."

"Are, too."

"I'm Jonah," a third boy piped up while the other two continued to disagree. "Jonah Bingham. You know my mom."

"Elaine," Griffin said, recalling the name of Stony's on-again, off-again lady friend, the one he seemed to be seeing more of than women he normally dated.

"Right."

"So who do your two argumentative friends belong to?" he asked, unable to prevent his smile at what he had deduced was an old argument between the twin boys.

"Those two are mine."

Griffin looked up to find that Sarah had rejoined the group, and his smile broadened at the picture of efficiency she presented in her Scouting outfit. He knew the last thing that should seem erotic to him was a den mother's uniform, but for some reason, her cool blue togs made his blood race. The chocolate was gone from her face, and her riotous curls had been brushed back and tamed by a simple leather headband. Yet the image of control and aloofness only made Griffin want to turn her as inside out as he was feeling himself.

Before he had a chance to comment further, the room began to fill with people, and amid a flurry of introductions and instructions to quiet down, the group was called to order. The rest of the evening passed in an atmosphere of barely controlled chaos, until every man present had been offered an opportunity to speak and answer questions about his occupation. Then the group dispersed to enjoy refreshments and mingle a little more.

All in all, Griffin enjoyed himself immensely. Normally he had little reason to be around kids beyond the occasional police-department function, and he recalled now how much he generally liked children. He wondered, as he inevitably did when confronted by kids, what it would be like to have one or two of his own.

Not for the first time, he reflected on the fact that Sarah's two sons shared last names different from hers, and he couldn't help but feel optimistic. She must be divorced, he decided. Unless, of course, she had never taken her husband's last name to begin with. He had noted almost immediately the absence of a wedding ring on her left hand, and no telltale indentation that one had ever been worn. Still, some people didn't wear wedding rings, so her lack of one was no surefire indication that she was single.

Of course, he could just come right out and ask her about her marital status, he reminded himself. But she would no doubt interpret the question as a social interest on his part—

which of course it was—and considering the fact that she was seventy-five dollars in the hole because of him, her reaction to his interest might not be as favorable as he'd like.

So instead Griffin contented himself by watching and wondering, and waiting for some cue from her. As the night began to draw to a close and he hadn't yet received one, he concluded he must have made a mistake earlier in the evening when she had studied him with such interest, and decided it might be best if he simply withdrew from the chase.

Until he looked up with the intention of telling her that it was time for him to go and saw her staring back at him with that strange, yearning expression a man would have to be a fool to misinterpret. She was as interested in him as he was in her. And Griffin decided then that there was no reason he had to leave just yet.

Sarah was nearly at her wit's end by the time the last mother left with the last child. Elaine offered to stay and help her clean up, but Sarah insisted she could manage on her own and sent her friend packing with Jonah. She wanted to be alone for a while, to contemplate her sanity and to wonder why on earth she had experienced such a major sexual awakening in the middle of a Cub Scout meeting.

All night long she had been unable to focus on anything except the way Officer Lawless's jodhpurs so lovingly fitted every hard plane of his lower body. It was criminal, really, how incredibly sexy that man looked in the uniform of a public servant. The only thing she had been able to think about all evening was what it would be like to indulge in raw, unbridled passion with him and his handcuffs. Lawless, indeed. No man had ever been named more appropriately.

As she tossed the last of the paper plates and cups in the trash, she listened vaguely to the sounds of her sons playing in Jack's room upstairs. That sound was followed by another, much closer—the whisper of creaking leather. Somehow it was a sound that didn't quite come as a surprise to Sarah. Somehow she had known Officer Lawless would still be in her house.

She turned to find him leaning oh-so-casually in the doorway between the kitchen and the dining room. He stood stock-still in all his cop regalia, eyeing her intently, his expression belying nothing of what he might be thinking. Sarah was still wondering how it would feel to lie naked and panting beneath him, and her breathing was a little shallow and ragged as a result.

"You're still here," she said quietly, her statement sounding silly in light of the obvious answer.

Yet it didn't prevent him from replying. "I hung back from the others. I thought maybe I could help you straighten up."

Sarah shook her head. "That's okay. There's not that much. Thanks for offering, though."

Instead of interpreting her assurance and thanks as an indication that it was time for him to leave now, Officer Lawless took two measured strides into the kitchen, pausing by the table.

"How come your sons have a different last name than you?" he asked.

His question didn't seem as odd as she might have thought under different circumstances, so she replied without hesitation. "They have their father's last name."

He nodded thoughtfully, then took a few more steps forward, his boots scraping quietly across the tile as he approached her. "And why don't you have their father's last name?" he asked further.

Sarah swallowed with some difficulty. With every step he took toward her, her pulse quickened with dangerous speed. "I took back my maiden name when I got divorced," she told him, unable to break her gaze free from his as he drew nearer.

"So you're single?"

He had come to a stop a scarce inch in front of her. Sarah nodded mutely in reply, unable to get words past the lump that was fast forming in her throat.

When he reached toward her face, she instinctively began to draw back. He seemed to notice her skittishness, because he frowned. Yet still his hand came forward, until his
fingers curled lightly over her throat and beneath her jaw.

"Officer Lawless," she began to object in a breathless
whisper.

"Griffin," he corrected her.

"Griffin. I don't think—"

"I've never seen a woman so prone to getting food on
herself," he interrupted her, drawing his thumb over the
corner of her mouth.

"What is it?" She tried once again to draw away.

But Griffin's touch followed her, until his thumb raked
across her lower lip. "There, that's got it," he told her
softly.

Before Sarah could reply, he was leaning forward, and
then his mouth was pressed against hers, his lips rubbing
gently over her own, the soft bristles of his mustache tick-
ling her skin. At first she was too surprised to respond, and
only stood before him, letting him kiss her. Then, when she
realized what was happening, she did indeed react with a
vengeance. Only instead of pushing him away, as her ra-
tional mind insisted she should do, her traitorous hands rose
to clutch at his shirt, her fingers somehow finding their way
to tangle in his hair.

And then Griffin responded, too, deepening the kiss until Sarah was pressed back against the kitchen counter, his
legs insinuating themselves between her own, his pelvis
pressing urgently against hers. The hand at her throat moved
to cradle the back of her head, tilting it until he could slant
his mouth more fully over hers. She felt another hand at her
waist, then on her ribs, until finally his warm palm curved
completely over her breast, rhythmically thumbing the peak
to expectant life. Sarah groaned at the electrical explosions
his touch set off on her skin, a sound that Griffin repeated
as he tasted her more deeply.

For long moments, the two struggled to see who could consume the other fastest, neither certain where their passion had come from or where it would lead. Sarah had settled her hand on the buckle of Griffin's belt when she heard something thump loudly upstairs. Immediately she remembered her sons and, with one savage gesture, pushed Griffin away.

At first she was unable to speak, so stunned was she by her behavior. All she could do was try to catch her breath and shake her head in silence, wishing more than anything in the world that she could turn back the clock five minutes and start all over again. But not because she wanted the outcome to be different, she realized to her dismay. Because she wanted to relive that kiss over and over again.

"Why... why did you do that?" she finally managed to whisper.

Griffin met her gaze levelly, his own breathing as ragged as hers. "Because you asked me to," he said.

Sarah shook her head in silent denial.

"You're doing it now, too," he told her. "Every time you look at me like that."

"But—"

"Mom! Jack hit me!"

"I did not!"

"You did, too!"

"Did not!"

"Did, too!"

Her sons' voices, raised in childish anger, awakened similar feelings in Sarah. She resented the way Griffin had so easily insinuated himself into her arms, was confused by her own willingness to let it happen and worried that she had so easily forgotten the presence of her children in the house. She was also angry as all get out that every nerve in her body was as aroused as hell thanks to Griffin Lawless. Consequently her words were edged with anger when she spoke.

"I think you'd better go."

"Have dinner with me tomorrow night."

Sarah wasn't sure what bothered her most—his ignoring her request that he leave; his stating, instead of asking, that she go out with him; or her own desperate desire to say yes.

"I can't," she told him.

"Why not?"

Not for the first time, she wished this night had never happened. Drawing in a deep breath, she met Griffin's gaze levelly and said reluctantly, "Because I already have a date." Roger, her claims adjuster, had talked her into going to a movie with him in exchange for his appearance tonight.

Griffin's expression changed drastically at her statement. "Oh. I see," he said, pushing himself away from her.

Sarah knew she should be grateful for the distance he seemed suddenly willing to place between them, but instead she felt inexplicably cold, despite the warm spring breeze sifting through the open window. When she felt herself wanting to explain the situation to Griffin, to ask him if maybe he was free Wednesday night, instead, Sarah forced herself to keep the words in check.

This was a man who had cost her seventy-five bucks she couldn't afford, she reminded herself. A man who was self-confident to the point of arrogance, who probably never heard the word *no* from a woman. What kind of message would she be sending him if she just jumped into his arms three days after he'd ticketed her for a crime she hadn't even committed?

Pushing aside the realization that that was precisely what she had just done, Sarah repeated her earlier statement. "I think you'd better go."

Griffin nodded silently and turned to leave, but she could tell her announcement that she was seeing someone else didn't sit well with him. Still, it was probably better this way. Never in her life had a man caused her so much turmoil in such a short time. Getting involved with Griffin Lawless would be dumb, she assured herself. He was too sexy, too overpowering, too authoritative, too everything. What she needed was a quiet man, an unassuming man, a safe man.

Like Roger, she thought blandly, waiting for even the slightest twinge of excitement the name might arouse.

Instead the only arousal that came was the one that hammered through her body as Sarah watched Griffin Lawless go out the door.

Three

——

"**Y**our first assignment, Griff. Make us all proud."

Griffin glanced up at Stony, then down at the manila folder the other man had tossed onto his desk. He smiled. "No sweat. What is it?"

"A contracting company here in Clemente called Jerwal, Inc.," Stony told him. "We've had the owners under surveillance for about three months now. There's reason to believe they're running a scam on some local businesses and private citizens. Gundersen and I put a lot of time in on this. I don't want to see it wasted."

Griffin shrugged. "Like I said, no sweat."

Stony nodded. "Read over the file and let me know if you have any questions. It's all pretty self-explanatory stuff. They don't know we've been watching them, but it's only a matter of time before we go public with this. A couple of months at most."

Griffin opened the manila folder and began to scan the information contained inside. The moment he saw the names of the two men he would be investigating, his palms grew damp, and his assurance of "No sweat" suddenly betrayed him. One of the men was named Jerry Schmidt, an inconsequential name, as Griffin had never heard of the guy. But the other man's name was Wallace Greenleaf. And in a town the size of Clemente, it was a pretty safe bet that anyone who carried that last name would be somehow related to Sarah.

He recalled the long spiel she had offered in explanation when he'd pulled her over two weeks ago. Hadn't she said something about going to meet a brother? he thought. He closed his eyes, thinking hard, trying to remember if the brother's name had been Wallace. He didn't think so. Wally, maybe? Griffin's eyes snapped open. That was it. Wally. Terrific.

He threaded his fingers through his hair, leaned back in his chair and stared at the ceiling. Well, he hadn't exactly expected to be seeing Sarah again socially, anyway, had he? Considering the less-than-promising origins of their acquaintance, and the fact that she had made it clear that night in her kitchen that she wanted nothing more to do with him, and her assertion that she was seeing someone else, this added little setback shouldn't be of any concern. Hell, he hadn't seen her for two weeks. There was no point in wanting to get close to her, anyway, right?

Wrong, he immediately answered himself. Considering the fact that he had been able to think of little other than the way she had felt melting into him in her kitchen two weeks ago, he had every reason to want to get close to her again. As close as a man could get to a woman without being burned alive.

Great. This was just great, he thought. He looked down at the file again and began to read, all the while wondering how he was going to work this out. It wasn't as if he could avoid Sarah. He had hired her and Elaine, after all. The two women were already invading his great-grandfather's house to appraise its contents.

How was he supposed to keep his hands off of her, when all he wanted was to drown one more time in her warmth and softness? He was already having trouble sleeping at night. Now, faced with certainly seeing Sarah again and wanting to know her better, and armed with the knowledge that he was investigating her brother for something that, if proven, could land the guy with a serious stint in jail, Griffin felt a little . . . well, lousy.

It figured, he thought. Just his luck. He'd managed to land the job he wanted and meet the potential woman of his dreams in the same week, and now it looked as though one would cancel out the other. How was he supposed to salvage something out of all this?

As he began to read the file once again, Griffin shook his head hopelessly, absolutely certain he heard all the gods laughing at him.

The Mercer house smelled musty, old and empty when Sarah entered it late in the afternoon two weeks to the day after she and Elaine had signed an agreement with Griffin Lawless. He had given them a key when he'd hired them so that they could come into the house while he was at work and begin the long process of cataloging and appraising the huge assortment of antiques Judge Mercer and his daughter had collected over the years. So far, only Elaine had come to the house, to survey its contents and estimate the size of the project the two of them were about to undertake. Sarah would begin the appraisal the following day and had decided to stop by on her way home to get a feel for the place, instead of entering it cold in the morning. Still, she crossed the threshold now with more than a little trepidation.

One of the main things that had drawn Sarah and Elaine together two years ago was a common affection for antiques. While Elaine's expertise lay in the area of furniture and jewelry, Sarah had always had an interest in and proficiency with serve ware—china, crystal, silver and linens.

When the two women had pooled their meager resources to purchase the antique shop in the historic section of Clemente, they had been seizing upon an opportunity neither had ever thought she would see. The owner, looking to retire, had put the establishment up for sale lock, stock and barrel, and because of his anxiousness to sell and escape to the balmier climate of Orlando, had agreed to a price that was quite beneficial to the two women.

They had added quite a bit more to their stock by taking in auctions throughout the Midwest, and they currently boasted a nice assortment of pieces. And although Sarah and Elaine weren't getting rich off of their new acquisition by any stretch of the imagination, they were managing to make ends meet. They looked forward to the summer ahead, when tourism thrived in historic Clemente, and were banking that they could make it through the lean winter off their fat take in the summer.

Naturally, any jobs they might encounter as appraisers only added to the till, and their current contract with Griffin Lawless was a real plum. The publicity alone could potentially double their business. Better than that, though—at least for Sarah—was the fact that she was finally going to have an opportunity to become utterly involved with the pieces she was inspecting.

She had loved antiques for as long as she could remember. Unfortunately, being the daughter of good—and poor—country people on both sides of her family, there were no Greenleaf heirlooms to speak of save the occasional hat pin or doll. Buying the business with Elaine had been a dream come true, but sometimes it hurt like hell to part with the items they stocked in the shop.

Sarah was fascinated as much by the history of a piece as by the skill used in creating it. And too often, pieces came and went too quickly for her to truly research their character and genesis. Certainly she knew quality when she saw it and could identify origins and manufacture, but she was seldom given the chance to trace an item back to its original owner or the circumstances for its coming into being.

Now she had the opportunity to really delve into an entire collection, one that no doubt spanned centuries. She could scarcely wait to get started.

"Hello?" she called out experimentally, unsure why she was bothering. Elaine had already told her there probably wouldn't be anyone home.

Griffin, she'd said, had offered no indication that he intended to move into the old house, nor had he bothered to be present when Elaine had come by the first time. The entire appraisal would take months, perhaps as long as a year, depending on the items in question. By trading off times they would work at the Mercer house, the two women were still able to run the shop, but Sarah's duties also meant she would be tied to Griffin Lawless for some time.

She had tried not to think about the kiss they had shared in her kitchen two weeks ago. Tried and failed miserably. Every time she closed her eyes at night, all she could see were Griffin Lawless's blue eyes filled with longing as he drew nearer, and all she could feel was the mind-scrambling heat that had shot through her body the moment he'd touched his lips to hers.

"Hello?" she called out again, hoping she imagined the nervous trill in her voice. "Is anybody home?"

The front-door hinges creaked ominously as she closed the door behind her, and Sarah couldn't help but be reminded of any number of Gothic novels she'd read as a teenager. Novels in which young, naive women succumbed to the seductions of dangerously sexy men in old, menacing houses where they were kept locked away.

She pushed the thought aside. She was neither young nor naive, and the Mercer house was anything but menacing. Of course, Griffin Lawless was dangerously sexy and appallingly seductive, but Sarah could handle herself there.

Hah! a little voice inside piped up unbidden.

Ignoring the little voice, she squared her shoulders resolutely, smoothed a few nonexistent wrinkles out of her sleeveless beige front-button sheath and strode forcefully into the house, hoping she exuded more confidence than she felt. The late-afternoon sun, slanting through windows that lined the wall above the front door, threw long beams of golden light across the entry hall. It reflected off scattering motes of dust as if fairies danced within. Dark wood paneling soared up twenty feet above Sarah in the entry hall, and a richly colored, very old Persian carpet cushioned her feet below. The house was every bit as beautiful as she had hoped it would be, and the thought of exploring its treasures made Sarah's blood race warm and lively.

To the left of the entry hall was a huge living room, while to the right was what appeared to be a sitting room or parlor. Between the two rooms, a wide staircase swept upward, separating into two sections that led to the second-floor gallery. Beside the stairs on the first floor, a long, mahogany-paneled hallway beckoned, so Sarah walked forward, her flat-heeled pumps echoing the leisurely pace of her footsteps.

The hallway ended in two French doors that were closed. Naturally curious, she reached for the brass handle of one and pushed it downward. The latch gave easily, and the door opened inward, almost of its own free will. The sweet scent of old books assailed Sarah then, and she smiled. A library. How wonderful.

The library was a repeat of the rest of the house—dark paneling, high ceilings, exquisite furnishings. She was standing in the center of the room, when she detected another aroma—that of a rich, expensive cigar. Her ex-husband had smoked them occasionally, and Sarah had always loved the fragrance. It was one of the few nice memories she carried of her marriage.

"So, Ms. Greenleaf, you've come at last."

She whipped around in panic at the masculine voice, even though she recognized it very well. Griffin Lawless sat in a leather-bound chair near the fireplace, looking very incongruous in the formal room. He wore extremely faded blue jeans, ripped across one knee, and a white, vee-neck T-shirt stretched taut over his muscular abdomen. He affectionately rolled a cigar between the thumb and index finger of one hand, while the other cradled a delicate crystal snifter of brandy. Sarah's heart hammered double-time at the picture he presented. She'd never seen a more striking man.

"I-I'm sorry," she stammered. "I would have knocked, but I, uh, I didn't realize anyone was here."

"No doubt," he quickly replied. "Had you realized I was here, you probably never would have come in."

Assuring herself that he was completely wrong, she said, "I won't be long. I was actually on my way home from the shop, but I wanted to come in and have a look around before I begin cataloging tomorrow."

Griffin nodded but said nothing in reply. His eyes never left hers as he placed the cigar in his mouth and inhaled deeply, holding the smoke in his lungs for several long moments before exhaling it in a slow spiral of white. Then, still watching her, he lifted his brandy to his lips for an idle sip, again swirling the liquor in his mouth to savor it before swallowing. The knowledge that he took such pleasure in sensual stimulation made Sarah's head spin, and she swallowed in vain to alleviate the dryness in her mouth.

"Drink?" he asked, lifting his glass in invitation, apparently noting her preoccupation.

She shook her head. "No, thanks. I haven't eaten since this morning, and it would go straight to my head."

Griffin wasn't sure that was such a bad thing, but he said nothing in reply. The thought of being present when Sarah Greenleaf lost control was oddly appealing. Why had this woman so thoroughly unsettled him? he wondered. Why did her face seem to be indelibly imprinted at the front of his brain? And why, dammit, could he think of little else other than the way her body had responded to his touch two weeks ago?

"So you'll be coming to the house, after all," he said. "I was beginning to think you were trying to avoid me."

"Me?" Sarah chirped with a high-pitched, anxious chuckle, diverting her gaze from his. "Why would I be avoiding you?"

Her nervousness was almost a palpable thing. Griffin smiled. "Because you've been thinking as much as I have about the manner in which we parted ways a couple of weeks ago."

Her eyes snapped to his again, and she inhaled deeply, the gesture making her breasts strain against the thin fabric covering them. His fingers twitched as he recalled the warm, soft flesh he had cupped briefly in his hand. Still clearly nervous, she began to fiddle with the top button of her dress, and his gaze fixed on the movement.

"I don't know what you mean," she said softly.

He placed the smoking cigar in a crystal ashtray on a side table, then set the snifter of brandy beside it and stood. Sarah took a giant step backward as he did so, so Griffin took a few giant steps forward to close the distance between them. His hand covered the one she had hooked into her buttonhole, while his other crept around her waist to press insistently at the small of her back until she was in his arms again. Then he kissed her, long and hard and deep, pulling back only when she uttered a soft sigh of surrender.

"Now do you remember?" he asked, his voice rough and ragged as he tried to tamp down his desire.

Sarah's breathing was a little raspy, but she managed to whisper, "Yes, I think it's coming back to me now."

He slanted his mouth over hers again, and she was lost in the smoky flavor of cognac and the sweet fragrance of tobacco that clung to him. Once again she felt the odd brush of his mustache above her lips and she tilted her head some to enjoy the full effect of his kiss. The hand covering hers loosened the button from her grasp and reached for the one below it, slipping the flat disk through the buttonhole before moving lower. When she realized Griffin had every intention of undressing her right there, Sarah finally managed to pull away, gripping his upper arms fiercely with her fingers as she held him at arm's length.

The fact that he allowed her to do so was simply a symbolic gesture, she knew. There was no way she was physically strong enough to hold him back. The muscles beneath her fingers were as hard and taut as bands of iron, the heat seeping from them into her flesh as searing as molten lava. For a long time she could only stare at him and fight for breath, and wonder how long this madness was going to last.

Griffin was too busy trying to gather his thoughts to wonder about anything for the moment. Sarah's dress gaped where he had managed to free three buttons, the champagne-colored lace of her camisole making him want to reach out and touch her again. Good God, what had come over him to start pawing at a woman he barely knew? He had to regain control of himself. This thing with Sarah Greenleaf was getting far too out of hand.

"Why do you do that?" she whispered after a moment. "Why do you just step up and take whatever you want without asking first?"

He shook his head silently, having no idea how to answer.

She dropped her hands to her sides, then lifted one to shove a handful of curls off her forehead. "This...this *thing* between us has to come to a stop right now, before it goes any further than it already has."

"Why?"

She stared at him incredulously. "Why?" she repeated.

Griffin nodded. "Why?"

She emitted a sound of disbelief. "Well, because..."

That scrap of creamy lace beneath her dress still taunted him, so he slowly strode forward and extended a hand toward it. When Sarah didn't flinch or try to move away, he touched a fingertip to the third button. He could see her pulse thumping wildly in her throat, and more than anything he'd ever wanted in his life, he wanted to undo the rest of the buttons and spread her dress open wide as he urged her body to the floor. Instead, with no small effort, Griffin forced himself to loop the button back through its hole, then repeat the gesture for the other two. But he couldn't resist tracing his thumb over her pulse before he pulled his hand away.

"Again, Sarah," he murmured, "I ask you why?"

It was the first time he had spoken her first name, and the sound of it coming from his lips made Sarah's heart do funny things.

"Because I'm not the kind of person who does things like that," she finally said.

One corner of his mouth lifted beneath the black mustache, an action she supposed was something of a smile. "Oh, no?" he asked.

"No," she insisted. "I'm not. Not usually, anyway. Usually I'm an incredibly normal, middle-class, suburban, divorced mother of two, whose life consists of the most mundane of tasks. Now, maybe I've been overextending myself for the past few months, but I'm not stressed out enough to do something totally crazy and self-destructive like get involved with a man like you."

"A man like me," he repeated. His jaw twitched in a barely perceptible way. "And just what kind of man is that?"

Sarah drew in a deep breath and shook her head slowly. "Look, never mind. I should go."

She turned to leave, but Griffin's voice halted her.

"Don't," he said quietly. "Don't go yet. It's kind of nice..." His voice trailed off, and he didn't complete his statement.

"What?" Sarah asked as she pivoted slowly around again.

"It's kind of nice having someone else here for a change." He rubbed the back of his neck restlessly and surveyed the big room. "This house is so empty. So lonely. As beautiful as this place is, I don't feel I belong here. I don't know that I'll ever be able to call this place home. It just doesn't feel like me."

Sarah's gaze followed his. As much as she hated to admit it, he didn't exactly look like the lord of the manor in his ragged jeans and T-shirt. He did, however, exude a raw power and confidence that commanded attention, something she was sure was a direct result of the Mercer genes. In that way, at least, Griffin seemed right at home in his surroundings.

"I've heard about what happened," she said, her quiet words sounding to her like thunder in the otherwise silent room.

His gaze locked with hers. "You mean about my mother being the lost Mercer," he said.

Sarah nodded. "When Elaine first told me you had inherited this place, I figured you must be related to an offspring of Judge Mercer's that I didn't know about. But Meredith was his only child, wasn't she?"

His expression was inscrutable as he said, "She was my grandmother and I didn't even know it."

Sarah tried to gauge Griffin's mood by the tone of his voice, but could detect nothing in the deep, resonant sound. Before she could comment, he continued.

"I found out about it just before Christmas. Apparently sometime around Thanksgiving the judge was overcome by a feeling of nostalgia and his own mortality and wanted to do right by the grandchild he'd never known."

He ran a hand through his hair and sighed. "The way the story came to me, Meredith Mercer was only fifteen when she fell in love with a boy from town who worked for the judge after school doing odd jobs. Needless to say, the old man wasn't too happy about the development, because the kid had no prospects, and he wanted something better for his daughter. When she got pregnant, the judge pretty much locked her in the house and brought in a tutor so no one would know. She had my mother when she was sixteen, and the judge immediately had the baby taken away and put up for adoption."

"The baby was your mother," Sarah said.

He nodded. "She was adopted by a couple from Cincinnati, and when she married my father, they moved to Clemente for his job. That's where the story becomes so ironic. For years, Meredith's daughter lived only a few miles away, yet neither ever knew it."

Griffin returned to his chair, picked up his cigar and inhaled deeply once again. He silently indicated the chair opposite his, and Sarah moved toward it. He seemed to want to talk about what had happened, and she had to admit she was curious. Not only about the story, but about his reaction to it. She couldn't help but wonder how all this made him feel. She couldn't imagine what it would be like to learn in her adult life that she had an entire family history she'd never known before.

After she seated herself, Griffin sat, too. "Do you blame him for everything?" she asked softly. "Judge Mercer, I mean."

He took another thoughtful sip of his brandy. "To be honest, I'm still not sure what I feel about this whole thing. I suppose he was as much a victim of circumstance as Meredith and my mother were. The times he lived in, the position he held in the community... I try to reassure myself he did what he thought was best. In the end, he did try to make amends."

After a moment, he added, "I would have liked to know my maternal grandfather, though. My mom's adoptive father had died by the time I was born. I'll never know what her birth father's name was. He might even still live here in Clemente. It's a strange feeling. Both my folks are gone now, and the family I never knew I had is gone, too. There might just be one other man out there I could call 'Gramps,' but I'll never know for sure."

"You don't have any brothers or sisters?" she asked.

He shook his head. "A handful of aunts and uncles and cousins scattered around, but I've never been particularly close to any of them."

"Family is important to you." Sarah's comment was a statement instead of a question, because she could already tell it was a fact.

"Yes, it is," Griffin told her. He studied her curiously. "Isn't it important to you?"

Sarah emitted a single, derisive chuckle. "You're talking to someone whose parents split after more than twenty years of marriage, telling me and Wally that they'd hated each other for most of those years and had only stayed married because of us kids. My brother and I get along about as well as a cobra and a mongoose. My own marriage was really over before it had a chance to begin, so maybe I'm not the person you should be asking that question."

"But you love your sons," he concluded.

"Of course I do," Sarah replied wholeheartedly. "But—"

"Then family is obviously important to you, too."

She thought for a moment, then began to smile. "Yeah, I suppose it is, now that you mention it. Funny, though, I never would have thought that before."

Griffin smiled back, and his face changed dramatically as a result. She hadn't thought him especially handsome. Attractive, yes. Striking, certainly. Sexy, by all means. But he was too rugged-looking to be handsome. Too rough around the edges. Too...too tough. But when he smiled that way... She sighed against her will. He was quite breathtaking.

"So which one are you?" he asked suddenly. "The cobra or the mongoose?"

Her brows drew downward in puzzlement. "What?"

"You said you and your brother get along as well as a cobra and a mongoose. I just wondered which one you are."

Sarah chuckled. "Oh, the mongoose, by all means," she said. "They're cuter."

"So they are," Griffin agreed, his smile broadening. Then, as suddenly as he had brightened, his expression became sullen again. "That would make your brother the cobra. A snake, so to speak."

She shrugged philosophically. "Wally's not a bad sort, really. He's just way too ambitious for his own good. It will ruin his life one day—mark my words."

He nodded again, and for a moment Sarah got the distinct impression that he knew something she didn't. Ridiculous, she assured herself. He was just preoccupied by thoughts of his own past.

"Look, I have to get going," she said as she rose from her chair. "My sitter only stays until six, and I'm sure it's almost that now."

Griffin glanced down at his watch. "Ten till," he told her.

Hastily she gathered up her things, trying to talk herself out of asking him the question she found herself so wanting to ask. Intending to tell him she would be back at the house in the morning to begin cataloging, what she actually said was "Do you have plans for dinner?"

When their eyes met, each could see clearly how surprised the other was by the question, and then they began to laugh.

"Actually, no, I don't," Griffin said, stubbing out his cigar. He lifted the brandy snifter to his lips and swallowed what little remained. "Why, Ms. Greenleaf, is that an invitation?"

She lifted a shoulder a little shyly but nodded. "Yes, I guess it is. Would you like to come home with me and join me and the boys for whatever is most convenient to thaw?"

"Love to."

As Griffin followed her out of the library and down the hall of his house—God, it still felt strange to think of the big building as such—he watched the subtle sway of her hips and the way she tossed her curls out of her eyes. He was supposed to be meeting Stony for dinner in an hour, he thought. He wondered if Sarah would mind if he used her phone once they got to her house.

Four

Sarah wasn't sure when she did it why she'd asked Griffin Lawless to join her and her family for dinner. Nor was she any closer to an answer later at her house, as she watched her sons make a huge fuss over him, demanding to know all about his motorcycle, asking what it was like to be a cop. Griffin had just looked so forlorn, so lost, sitting there in the Mercer library, she recalled now. She hadn't been able to resist.

She'd always been a sucker for stray animals. And maybe that's exactly what he had become to her. A stray animal who wasn't quite certain how to handle the blows the world was dealing him. She, on the other hand, was no stranger to unfair experiences. And if her experience in handling them could maybe help Griffin in some way, then she was obliged to take him under her wing, right?

The only problem was that this particular stray was far more dangerous than any other Sarah had ever brought home. This one was a predator, pure and simple, and somehow she wasn't quite sure she would be able to escape him should he set his sights on her. Would she be taking him under her wing? she wondered. Or would he wind up making a meal out of her first?

"Mom, can we go for a ride on Griffin's bike?" Jack asked.

Sarah stood on the front porch and eyed the big motorcycle dubiously. "I don't think so, sweetie," she said decisively. "Maybe when you're a little older."

"Aw, Mom..."

"And you should address Officer Lawless as 'Officer Lawless,'" she added when she realized how familiar the boys were already becoming with Griffin.

"But he's not an officer anymore," Sam joined in. "He just told us so."

"Of course he is," Sarah said, realizing guiltily that she hadn't followed much of the conversation because she'd been too preoccupied with thoughts about the man in question. "He's—"

"I'm actually Detective Lawless now," Griffin told her with a sheepish grin. "I got promoted a couple of weeks ago. Sorry I didn't tell you earlier. It just didn't come up in conversation."

She felt a momentary tug of regret when she realized she wouldn't be seeing him in his cute little motorcycle outfit anymore, but tried to remain philosophical. Detectives still carried handcuffs, didn't they?

The wayward thought caused her to stumble over her next words. "Oh. I see. Uh, well, then. Then you should call Officer Lawless 'Detective Lawless,'" she told her sons, hoping none of them saw the blush she felt creeping up from her toes to her hairline. "I mean, you should call *Detective* Lawless 'Detective Law—'"

"Really, 'Griffin' is fine," he interrupted her. "There's no reason to stand on ceremony."

Jack and Sam beamed at him, clearly suffering from a severe case of hero worship all over again. Sarah hoped she hadn't done the wrong thing in bringing Griffin home. She didn't want her sons to get used to having him around, any more than she wanted to get used to that herself. It was probably too late, though, she realized as she watched Griffin help Sam sit on the big motorcycle, steadying her son with one hand, the bike with the other. Too late for the boys, anyway. Certainly she could keep herself in line. Couldn't she? Of course she could.

With one final, worried look over her shoulder, she entered the house. "I'll just start dinner, why don't I?" she said through the screen door.

"Sounds great," Griffin replied, smiling at her before turning to address a question Jack asked him about something called "c.c.s."

As she searched through the eclectic assortment of prepackaged food in her freezer, Sarah pondered her almost daily concern about whether Jack and Sam were getting all the masculine attention they needed. Michael hadn't sought custody of his sons when the couple had divorced, but he had been granted liberal visitation. The boys spent a month every summer with him—and now with his new wife, too, Sarah remembered—not to mention an occasional weekend here and there. But Michael and Vivian lived in Pennsylvania now, so he wasn't close by if the boys ever needed him in a pinch.

And those pinches had been coming more and more frequently as Jack and Sam got older. They had questions now that Sarah was certain would be answered much more appropriately by a man, but there just weren't any men in her life she trusted with the boys in that way. She wouldn't even let Wally spend time alone with them lest he infect them with his aggressive workaholic philosophy. She wanted her sons to enjoy their childhoods and make the most of every moment of every day, and she'd done her best to see that they did. But she couldn't help thinking that little boys needed strong male role models, just as little girls needed strong women to inspire them. Sarah knew she was a good mother.

But it was tough trying to be the father Jack and Sam needed, too.

Her attention was caught by the sound of Sam's laughter erupting outside the open window. She smiled. The boys had taken to Griffin immediately at their Cub Scout meeting. He had clearly captivated the entire group much more completely than any of the other men had. And when the two boys had come barreling out the front door tonight to discover their mother had brought Officer—or rather, Detective—Lawless over again, they had been clearly delighted.

Sarah pulled a family-size bag of chicken breasts out of the freezer, then located a big bag of ready-to-mix, stir-fry vegetables. If something had to be microwaved more than fifteen minutes or boiled more than twelve, there was a good chance it wouldn't be found in her kitchen. She wished she were one of those women who could work all day without mussing her hair, stop by the market on the way home and come breezing through the door with fresh everything, throw it in a pot and whip up a gourmet feast in fifteen minutes flat.

"Hah," she muttered as she wrestled with one of the plastic bags to open it. "Women who can do that always wind up in the loony bin before their thirty-fifth birthdays."

Tossing the frozen assortment onto the counter, Sarah went to work. Maybe she wasn't the most organized woman in the world, but she could sure whip up a mean stir-fry at a moment's notice.

As she prepared dinner, she wondered again about the immediate union her sons had seemed to strike with the compelling Detective Lawless. Must be something in the Greenleaf genes, she thought. Because as much as she dreaded to admit it, she'd struck something of an immediate union of her own with the man. And where the boys would probably end up with a friend for life in Griffin, she couldn't help but wonder—and worry about—what her relationship with the man might wind up being.

She had a good appetite. Griffin watched in silent admiration as Sarah piled a third helping onto her plate. Of course, he remembered she'd told him that she hadn't eaten since morning, but most women, when dining with a man for the first time, would probably have been less willing to let him know how completely they could put their food away. But Sarah Greenleaf made no apology for being hungry. Griffin liked that. It made him wonder what other appetites she had, and whether those appetites were as voracious and slow to be satisfied as this one clearly was.

"So how come you're not a motorcycle cop anymore?" Jack, who was seated to Griffin's left, asked around a mouthful of food.

He looked down into the pale amber eyes of the eight-year-old and smiled. The two boys were like color negatives of each other—Jack with his dark curls and light eyes, and Sam with golden hair and eyes the color of coffee. They were opposites in other ways, as well, he'd noted. Jack was the outgoing one, almost showmanlike in the way he presented himself. Sam, on the other hand, seemed content to hang back a bit. Certainly he had no qualms about piping up when he wanted to know something, but, like his mother, he tended to wait and see what would happen before plunging in.

They had good names, too, Griffin thought. Jack and Sam. Straightforward, solid, old-fashioned names, completely at odds with the recent yuppie habit of selecting upscale, trendy and sometimes bizarre-sounding monikers. He wondered briefly whether Sarah or her ex-husband had chosen the names, and decided almost immediately it must have been Sarah. She was simply straightforward, solid and, yes, a bit old-fashioned, too.

"I'm not a motorcycle cop anymore," he said when he remembered he'd been asked a question that required an answer, "because I thought detective work would be a lot more interesting. And a lot more fun."

"Do you still get to have a gun?" Sam asked.

"Sam . . ." Sarah groaned.

Griffin smiled. Clearly she was none too happy about her son's preoccupation with firearms. "Yes, I do," he said.

Sam's eyes brightened. "Do you have it with you now?" he asked.

Griffin shook his head. "Nope. It's locked up. It's not a toy, Sam. Not something to be carried around by just anyone. Guns should only be allowed into the hands of those who are responsible enough and smart enough to know how to use them. And that doesn't include very many people, I'm afraid. Mostly law-enforcement officers. Few others."

The little boy's face fell. "Does that mean you won't teach me how to shoot it?"

Griffin glanced up at Sarah for a moment, already knowing how he would answer the question, but wanting to communicate he respected her wishes, too. "No, Sam, I won't. Guns don't belong in the hands of children."

Sarah relaxed, throwing him a small, grateful smile. He smiled back.

"See?" Jack said, wadding up his napkin to throw it at his brother, seated opposite him at the table. "I told you Griffin wouldn't have his gun with him."

"You did not," Sam shot back.

"I did, too."

"Did not."

"Did, too."

"Boys," Sarah interrupted. "If you're finished with your dinner, why don't you go outside and play? It's a lovely evening tonight, and tomorrow it's supposed to rain."

Two chairs scraped away from the table, and the boys continued to argue through the kitchen toward the back door.

Sarah shook her head mutely as she watched them leave. Seeming to remember something suddenly, she called out, "And don't slam the door on your way—"

The back door slammed shut behind them with a vigorous shudder.

"Out," she concluded with a soft sigh.

She looked at Griffin and shrugged. "Boys," she said simply, as if that explained everything.

He nodded. "I was exactly the same way when I was a kid. The only difference was that I didn't have brothers or sisters to fight with. I had to grapple with the neighborhood kids instead."

"You sound like you miss not having had a sibling," Sarah said as she stood to clear the plates. "How ironic. I spent most of my youth wishing I were an only child."

Griffin rose to help, but she gestured him back down. "You can help me with the dishes later," she told him. "I think I'd like some coffee first. How about you?"

"Coffee sounds great."

As Sarah went about the motions, Griffin watched, marveling at what a good time he was having doing almost nothing at all. He smiled at her matter-of-fact assurance that he would help with the dishes. By feeding him dinner, she'd made it clear he was a guest in her home—but not so formal a guest that he wouldn't be expected to pull his own weight. Her frankness was something else he liked about her. Sarah Greenleaf was different from most women he knew. And her differences intrigued him.

"I can't imagine growing up an only child, though," she said when she returned to the table. This time she ignored the seat she had previously occupied opposite his, and instead sat in the chair to his left that Jack had just vacated. "Even though Wally and I didn't get along a lot of the time, there were moments when the two of us could get beyond our sibling rivalry and have fun together. Christmases were always especially nice. Wally would help me figure out how my new toys worked, showed me how to put in the batteries or read the instructions to me when I was too young to read. And on Halloween, he always held my hand when we went trick-or-treating and ignored the bigger boys who razzed him about being stuck with his kid sister."

Griffin grunted noncommittally. He didn't want to hear anything nice about Wallace Greenleaf, didn't want to know what a protective brother he had been. In order to shift the conversation away from the man he was investigating, he said, "It really wasn't so bad being an only child. I was always the center of attention and never had to share anything. I never had to fight with my brother or sister over who had dibs on the TV or stereo, and I had a room all to myself. But sometimes . . ."

"Sometimes?" Sarah said, encouraging him to continue.

He shrugged. "Sometimes I wonder how it would have been to have someone else around. Especially now that both my parents are gone. It's strange, being the last of the Lawless line." After a moment, he added, "And now evidently the last of the Mercers, too."

Sarah watched Griffin closely, wondering what he was thinking about. This was the second time today their conversation had turned to the subject of family, and she couldn't recall on either occasion what had caused the topic to arise. Perhaps it was simply foremost in his mind right now, she thought. Certainly the recent turn of events in his life would warrant a rethinking of what family meant.

The coffeemaker wheezed as it gasped out the last few drops of the dark brew, and Sarah rose to fill two generous mugs. She returned to the table, offered him cream and sugar and, when he shook his head, sat down again. She drank hers black, too.

"Did you really become a detective because you thought it would be more interesting?" she asked. "More fun? I'd think riding around on a motorcycle all day would be better than sitting behind a desk in a crowded, poorly ventilated office."

He had lifted the mug to his lips, but hesitated as he thought about her question. After a deep swallow, he smiled. "You know, that's a strange comment coming from a woman who's out seventy-five dollars because of my riding around on a motorcycle all day."

When Sarah made a face at him, he chuckled, a deep, rusty sound that seemed to erupt from the very depths of his soul. A thrill of something warm and unfamiliar ran down her spine, and as much as she wished she could toss off a witty comeback, her mind was a complete blank. Only the rich, rumbling echo of his laughter resounded like a warm wind.

When she didn't reply, Griffin continued, "I was never given a court date, so I can only assume you paid your fine." His eyes sparkled like pale blue diamonds. "Unless of course I missed it somehow and you didn't show, and now they've issued a bench warrant for your arrest. In which case, Ms. Greenleaf, I'm going to have to run you in."

How could he make such a playful threat sound like such an incredibly erotic promise? Sarah wondered. "That won't be necessary," she said in a shallow voice. "I paid the fine. It just seemed easier and less time-consuming. Of course, now I won't be able to get that big book on Baccarat crystal I was saving up for, but..."

"I'll make it up to you," Griffin told her.

From the tone of his voice, she was afraid to ask what he had in mind for repayment. Instead she told him, "You already have by hiring Elaine and me to appraise the judge's collection."

His face clouded a bit at the mention of the man who had prevented him from knowing so much about himself. He dropped his gaze to stare down into his coffee, seeing something Sarah was sure she wouldn't see herself. Before their conversation could be steered to a subject he probably wanted to avoid, she jumped back to the one she had meant to raise earlier. "So why did you really become a detective?"

She wasn't sure, but she thought Griffin looked grateful when his eyes met hers again. "A few months ago, I was shot in the line of duty," he told her bluntly.

She flinched at his statement, spilling hot coffee over the side of her cup. "Shot?" she asked, a soft whisper all she was able to manage.

He nodded, but seemed less concerned than she was herself. "In the shoulder," he said, lifting a hand absently to the body part in question, rolling the shoulder as if testing it. "It wasn't life-threatening, but it made me ... reevaluate ... a few things. I decided detective work would be less dangerous." He dropped his hand back to the handle of his coffee cup. "Let's face it. Riding around on a motorcycle all day isn't exactly safe in itself. Add to that the dangers that go along with police work anyway, and you have a real good combination for bringing on a premature end to life."

Sarah opened her mouth to ask more, but Griffin stopped her with a question of his own.

"How long have you been divorced?" he asked.

It took a moment for her brain to adjust to the change of subject, but she eventually replied, "A little over three years now."

"Does your husband still live in Clemente?"

Griffin told himself his curiosity was nothing more than a desire to divert the conversation away from himself. Unfortunately, he knew such an assurance was untrue. He wanted to know all about Sarah's past and present and, worse, wanted to help her make plans for the future. It wasn't a good idea, he tried to tell himself. Not only was he investigating her brother—a fact she might find less than appealing—but she simply wasn't the kind of woman with whom he should find himself mixed up. She just wasn't his type.

So why the intense attraction? he wondered. And just why hadn't he told her about the investigation? Doing so would certainly precipitate an end to their time together, wouldn't it? If that was what he wanted, why didn't he just tell Sarah her brother was under investigation for bilking half the town and be done with it?

He tried to assure himself that he didn't tell her because it was against police procedure. She might tip her brother off, after all, and Wally would undoubtedly start trying to cover his tracks, something that would make Griffin's job more difficult than it already was. A simple response for a simple question.

But somehow things just didn't seem that easy. Griffin had a feeling he was less concerned about Sarah tipping her brother off than he was about the fact that she would be out of his own life faster than a streak of lightning if she found out about the investigation. And although being done with her was precisely what he *should* want first and foremost, it was in fact the last thing he wanted.

For some reason, he wanted to keep Sarah close at hand for as long as he possibly could. At least until he figured out what the hell was going on between them. And for that reason, not the more logical professional one, he decided to keep his mouth shut on the subject of her brother. Unless she came right out and asked him point-blank if he had on his desk a file that specifically mentioned Wallace Greenleaf. He wasn't sure if he could lie to her flat out.

He realized then that Sarah was speaking, and shook his errant thoughts from his brain to focus on their conversation once again.

"Michael remarried a few months ago and moved to Pittsburgh, where his new wife works. It's kind of funny, really," she added, staring at some point past Griffin's shoulder, "how he could never accommodate a single request *I* made while we were married, but he left his job, his home, his children, his whole life here to make her happy."

Realizing how bitter she sounded, Sarah tried to smile. "I shouldn't complain, though. Divorcing Michael was probably the smartest thing I ever did."

"What went wrong?" Griffin asked.

She sighed, toying with her coffee cup, for some reason unable to meet his gaze. "Probably we never should have married in the first place. I was still in college and wanted to graduate before we tied the knot. Michael talked me out of it, talked me into getting married, instead. For a couple of years I didn't do anything except be 'Mike's wife.' I thought about going back to school, but about the time I decided to enroll, I realized I was pregnant."

Sarah smiled then. "Jack and Sam are wonderful—they've always been good kids. I wouldn't trade them for anything. But Michael kept me so stifled after they were born. Don't get me wrong," she hastened to add. "I honestly don't think he did it consciously. Certainly he was never mean or patronizing. He just didn't want me doing anything except raising the boys."

"And that wasn't enough for you?" Griffin asked.

Sarah finally looked up, thrust out her chin defensively and stared him right in the eye. "No, I'm afraid it wasn't. God knows I love being a mother. But I have to have something else, too. Is that so terrible?"

He shook his head. "Not if it's what you want."

She gazed down at her hands again. "I guess I was happy enough when Jack and Sam were little and needed me. But once they started school, started becoming more independent, I wanted to put my energies into something else that needed me. Michael just never could understand that. Of course, he had a career that demanded his attention almost twenty-four hours a day."

"And now you have that, too," Griffin concluded.

She nodded. "A career, anyway, though not one that commands so much of me that I have time for little else. The antique business with Elaine has been perfect. With both of us being single mothers, we understand each other's needs, and we can swap duties and juggle our time. It's worked out very well."

"Elaine certainly seems to know what she's doing," Griffin said. He leaned forward in his chair, resting his elbows on the table and tucking his hands under his arms. The motion brought his face to within inches of hers, and she forced herself not to pull back. "And now, Sarah," he continued, a suggestive smile tugging at his lips, "I guess I'll get to find out if you know your stuff as well."

His quiet voice set her pulse to racing and her heart thumped madly behind her rib cage at the look on his face when he'd made his comment. Why did she suddenly feel as if "knowing her stuff" encompassed far more than her command of her job? Without her realizing it, Griffin Lawless had become a very important part of her life. Not only was he a client who would probably be responsible for turning her business around, but he was a man she was beginning to find more and more attractive, despite the questionable way in which she had met him.

She had thought it bad enough that her encounter with the infuriating Officer Lawless would cost her seventy-five dollars. Now she was beginning to wonder if the expense would be far, far greater than that, a price higher than she could afford and in no way connected to a monetary amount. And suddenly she began to worry that paying this fine might just do her in completely.

Five

"Sarah, you're passing up the chance of a lifetime here."

Sarah stared at her brother blandly as she withdrew a bunch of broccoli from a brown paper grocery bag and stowed it in the vegetable crisper. His coloring was similar to hers, but he had lost vast amounts of his curly hair, and his scalp shone brightly beneath what little was left. The spare tire around his middle seemed to be inflating a little more every time she saw him, and she wondered if he was still seeing Dr. Rowan for his blood pressure. She knew better than to ask, however. Wally was nothing if not confrontational where his health was concerned.

"Wally," she began, trying to hold on to her patience. Why did he always stop by on Saturday mornings, when she had a million things to do? "You know better than this. You know I'm having trouble making ends meet now. The shop is just barely turning a profit, and I don't have any money lying around to invest in some risky scheme of yours."

"This isn't a risk, Sarah—it's a sure thing. You'd be making an excellent investment."

She glared at him doubtfully. "A roller-blade rink for toddlers doesn't sound like a sure thing to me. It sounds like something only an idiot or a swindler would promote."

Wally looked absolutely flabbergasted. "Why, Sarah, how could you say such a thing about your own brother? You wound me. These roller rinks are the wave of the future." He paused for only a moment before launching into another idea. "Okay, if you don't like that project, how about this one? A topless cafeteria. All the servers would be nude."

Her quick, efficient movements came to a halt, and she turned around to gape at her brother. "You have got to be kidding."

He shook his head, beaming. "Isn't it a great idea? I came up with it myself. Think of the appeal to conventioneers. Cheap eats, naked girls, everything a man wants when he's on the road. Puts Jell-O salad into a whole new perspective, doesn't it?"

Sarah shook her head ruefully. Wally was such a jerk. She couldn't believe the two of them had resulted from the same gene pool. "Now, you *do* know better than to ask me to invest in something like that. Even if I did have the money, which I don't. Wally, you should be ashamed of yourself. What would Mom think?"

"Mom's in for ten grand."

She rolled her eyes heavenward. "Well, I'm not in at all."

"All right, all right, I won't ask you about my projects again unless you come to me first," he promised her. "But you know, you wouldn't be in such dire financial straits if you had stayed married to Michael. The guy was worth a bundle."

Sarah sighed fitfully. So they were back to that again, were they? She knew it was pointless to argue with her brother, but she simply could not let his comment go unanswered. "First of all, Michael wasn't worth a bundle."

"He pulled in seventy-five thou a year."

"Which I hate to tell you, dear brother, isn't as much as it sounds like when you've got a mortgage, two cars and the care, feeding and future of two kids to think about. Second of all, what happened between me and Michael is none of your business. And third," she said, hurrying on before he could object, "you spend an awful lot of time speculating on my marriage, when you've never even come close to making a commitment like that yourself. If you're so keen on the institution of matrimony, how come you're still a single guy? Now, I know a woman who would love to go out with you—"

"Gosh, is that clock right?" Wally interrupted, jumping up from his lazy position at her kitchen table. "I didn't realize it was getting so late. Gotta run."

He kissed her quickly on the cheek and then dashed out the back door. Sarah heard the rumble of his sports car, then the squeal of tires as he hightailed it out of her driveway. She smiled. Yes, her brother was annoying sometimes. But she knew exactly how to handle him when he started to overstep the bounds. She should be careful, though. Someday he was going to call her on that "I know a woman" business and ask to be introduced. Frankly Sarah didn't know anyone who was interested in meeting Wally, despite her best efforts to fix him up. Still, that didn't mean she had to stop trying.

She hummed softly as she put the rest of her groceries away, scarcely noting that the song she'd chosen was something about highways and adventure and motorcycle riders who were born to be wild.

It was nearly a week later when Sarah saw Griffin again. She was standing at the center of an attic in the Mercer house, hip deep in opened crates, with dust and bits of straw swirling madly about her. A bare bulb swinging laconically above her provided the only illumination in the cramped, slant-ceilinged room, and she was hot. Her perspiration-soaked, red T-shirt clung to her like a wet animal, and her faded jeans felt loose, as if she'd sweated off ten pounds since morning. Yet her discomfort did little to distract her.

Because she had found a treasure.

Each of the crates contained a cache of fine china, every bit of it representative of a generation in the Mercer family. Some of the pieces dated back at least two hundred years, most of the collection was European in manufacture and all of it was in exquisite shape, with more than a few museum-quality pieces.

Why was all of this packed away? she wondered. Why was none of it in use? Or on display? If the Mercers had no longer felt any need for it, why hadn't they arranged for others to enjoy it? There must be tens of thousands of dollars' worth of china here alone. And, she reasoned further, there was probably crystal, and perhaps silver, to match these assortments, as well. Where were those?

She shook her head in wonder that one family had amassed such a collection. She couldn't imagine what Griffin would want to do with all this. Sell it, most likely, she decided. Truly, that was probably the most logical thing for him to do. Still, it seemed a shame no one would use any of this to entertain anymore. At one time the Mercer home must have been filled with people for holidays and family gatherings. Whoever had been madam of the house then would have made certain all the nicest of her pieces were polished and piled high with food. This old place must have been lovely in its heyday, Sarah thought. Too bad it hadn't seen much life for the past several decades.

She wondered if Griffin would sell the house. Probably. It was a large residence by contemporary standards, especially for one person. And despite their talks about the importance of family, he didn't seem the type to settle down and have a passel of kids. No doubt the house would go on the block, just as everything inside would. The sale of his newly inherited belongings would bring Griffin a tidy sum, to be sure, but somehow, she didn't think he was the type to be much changed by his wealth.

She bent down to reach into another crate and withdrew a stunning piece of Limoges. She skimmed her fingertips over the creamy china, tracing the cobalt stain and gold trim. Bernardaud, she decided before allowing herself to inspect the marking. Probably about a hundred years old. Flipping the dinner plate over to read the bottom, she confirmed her assumption. She turned to carefully place the piece beside another that matched it, and when she pivoted around, saw a large figure looming in the doorway.

Griffin filled a room without even entering it, she thought as he stood there without speaking. Instinctively she lifted a hand to smooth over her hair, cursing herself for caring how she looked in his presence. The perspiration-soaked curls sprang right back when she removed her hand, and Sarah saw bits of straw clinging to her fingers. Oh, great. She must look really terrific with straw and dust sticking to every last inch of her.

"Aren't you hot up here?" he asked by way of a greeting.

His standard uniform of ragged jeans and T-shirt had been replaced by loose-fitting cotton khakis, rumpled white shirt, nondescript, neutrally colored jacket and a skinny, outdated necktie that must have belonged to his father. He looked like a combination of Columbo and Joe Friday. But his blue eyes burned in the stark light provided by the naked bulb, and Sarah felt her temperature rise even more. Hot? Yeah, she was hot. But it had nothing to do with the oppressive heat of a southern Ohio summer.

"Just a little," she said, hoping her voice sounded less limp than she felt.

He crossed the threshold and approached her slowly, ignoring the mess she'd made to focus on her instead. With every step he took toward her, Sarah found it more difficult to breathe. By the time he came to a halt before her, her lungs felt empty. He lifted a hand and curved it around her neck, rubbing his thumb along her jaw. When he pulled his hand away, she could see that his fingers were wringing wet. When he picked a piece of straw from her hair, he smiled.

"You don't look just a little hot," he told her. "You look like you're about to dehydrate. Come on downstairs. I'll fix you something cool to drink."

He turned then and began to walk out, and the crazy moment that had tied Sarah in a knot passed as quickly as it had begun. She had no choice but to follow him, because suddenly all she wanted was to be close to him again.

Griffin was already standing in front of the open refrigerator door by the time Sarah caught up with him. He called himself a fool for having run out on her that way, but if he'd stayed up there with her a minute longer, he would have done something he shouldn't. Like tumble her to the floor and have his way with her. She'd just looked so damned sexy up there in her tight, wet T-shirt with no brassiere underneath. He'd seen every curve and shadow of her breasts as if she'd been wearing nothing at all, and he'd wondered if her lower extremities were as intriguing.

When he turned to find her standing scarcely a foot away from him, still damp, still sexy as hell, he realized coming downstairs into the air-conditioning hadn't helped at all. He still wanted her. Only now, he wanted her even more.

"There's soda or beer," he told her, forcing himself to concentrate on the contents of his refrigerator instead of the way her blue jeans hung low on her hips. "Which do you prefer?"

"Actually, ice water sounds better than anything," she said, swiping again at her damp curls.

Griffin nodded, pulled some ice from the freezer and went to the sink. Instead of emptying the tray, he withdrew only a few cubes, tossed them into a glass and filled it with water from the tap. Sarah took it and drank thirstily, and he watched, fascinated, how her throat worked over the swallows.

"Thanks," she said when she had drained the glass.

"More?"

She nodded, handing the glass back.

When she did so, Griffin's hand closed over hers for a moment longer than was necessary. He had promised himself he wasn't going to do this. That he wouldn't be so fascinated by her, so wrapped up in thoughts of her, so affected by her presence. The more he uncovered in his investigation of Jerwal, Inc., the more he was convinced Wallace Greenleaf was into some pretty shady dealings. It wouldn't be fair—not to mention ethical—to court Sarah while he was trying to put her brother behind bars.

But as he pulled his hand away from hers, he knew it was pointless even to try to stay away from her. There was something burning up the air between them—that much was undeniable. And judging by the look in her eyes, she was as eager as he was to explore the attraction further.

Sarah slowly sipped her second glass of water as Griffin put the ice away. She wondered what he was thinking about. Ever since he'd come in, he'd been looking at her as though she was something worth looking at. An awkward silence loomed between them, and for the life of her she had no idea what to say to end it. The only thoughts that popped into her head now were of the physical variety, and all included Griffin Lawless. To speak now might make her say—or do—something she'd regret later.

"How's it coming?" he asked, and she hoped her sigh of relief wasn't audible.

"Very well," she told him. "I've discovered some wonderful things upstairs."

He nodded, but said nothing more. Just as she'd suspected, he obviously wasn't overly concerned about the enormous collection that now belonged to him.

"How long do you think it will take to get everything itemized?"

"Still hard to say, really. There's another attic on the other side of the house, and I haven't even looked inside it yet."

He nodded again, seemingly satisfied. "You busy tomorrow night?"

Sarah had been ready for more queries about the progress of her work, and this question threw her for a moment. The last time they had been alone together was when he had eaten dinner at her house. The evening had ended awkwardly, with the two of them parting ways at the front door while Jack and Sam watched TV only a few feet away. There had been a palpable tension in the air. Sarah had been thinking about the kisses they had shared earlier in the afternoon, and had known Griffin was remembering them, too. As much as she hated to admit it, she had been wanting to kiss him again. She should have been thankful the boys were there to prevent something like that. Instead she had wanted to pack them off to bed early.

Right now, of course, her sons were nowhere near her and Griffin. Right now, if she wanted, Sarah could step forward and plant a kiss on him that he wouldn't likely forget. But she only shook her head and said, "No, I'm not busy tomorrow night. Why?"

Griffin shrugged, but she could tell that the gesture was anything but casual. "There's a softball game then. The men and women in my precinct—the first precinct—are playing the second precinct. It's a grudge match. They took the city tournament from us last year." He seemed to be preoccupied by an old stain on the kitchen counter as he added, "I just wondered if you and the boys might want to come and watch."

She smiled. "Jack and Sam would love it."

"And their mother?" he asked as he looked up to meet her gaze. "Would she love it, too?"

Sarah caught her breath at the expression of utter longing in his eyes, fearful that what she saw was nothing more than a reflection of her own desire. Without hesitation, she replied, "Yes, Griffin, she would. She's probably looking forward to it more than the boys will."

He suddenly seemed relieved for some reason. "Good. I have to get back to work—I just came home on my lunch hour to see how you were getting along. How about if I pick you all up around five tomorrow? We can grab a quick bite to eat on the way."

Sarah's gaze lingered on the clock hanging on the wall behind Griffin. Only twenty-eight and a half hours stood between her and five o'clock tomorrow. She could probably stand being alone until then. Probably. "Five will be fine. We'll be ready."

He pushed away from the counter and began to walk past her, then stopped. Turning back around, he lifted a hand to her cheek and smiled, then bent forward and brushed his lips softly, swiftly, over hers. "See you tomorrow," he said quietly as he left.

Sarah raised two fingers to her lips, as if in doing so, she might be able to preserve the lingering effect of the kiss. But as quickly as Griffin was gone, so was the sensation. She told herself she should remember that pleasure was always a fleeting thing. Instead she couldn't stop grinning for the rest of the afternoon.

"Eh, batter, batter, batter, batter...suh-*wing*, batter."

As Griffin poised himself in right field, he shook his head and smiled. Sarah stood in the stands with her palms flattened over her eyes against the glare of the setting sun, doing everything within her power to annoy the opposing team. Every time a member of the second precinct approached home plate to bat, she was there chattering like a Little League mother, trying her best to blow the batter's concentration. Jack and Sam sat on each side of her, as intent on the game as she was herself.

He knew she'd be the type to balk at being called cute, but...she sure was cute. Her unruly curls smashed out from beneath a navy blue ball cap identical to the ones his team wore and that Sarah had donned backward. Her cropped white T-shirt offered a tantalizing glimpse of tanned torso, and faded cutoffs showcased her long, bronzed legs.

"Ball?" she yelled through the chain-link fence at the umpire. "Ball? What are you, blind? That was a strike, even in my grandma's time. How can you call that a ball? Kill da ump!"

Griffin chuckled. She was nothing if not enthusiastic about her sports.

The thump of a bat brought his attention around, and he looked up to find a softball descending in a perfect arc toward him. He caught the pop fly easily, then glanced over at third base in time to catch Denny Malloy trying to steal a run, so he hurled the ball home. When the dust settled, and the umpire called the runner safe, Griffin rolled his eyes heavenward, waiting for what he knew would come next.

"Safe?" Sarah shouted. "What are you, nuts? Here, pal. Here's a quarter! Call the home for demented umpires and book yourself a padded room, 'cause you're crazy! The guy was out by a mile!"

"Hey, Lawless," Stony called out from his position at shortstop. "Looks like you got yourself a live one there."

Griffin grinned back at his friend, lifted his cap and swept back his damp hair before putting the cap on again. "Yeah, she is that," he said with a sigh.

The two teams waited patiently while Sarah and the umpire engaged in a brief, but heated, difference of opinion. Griffin watched with his hands settled casually on his hips as the umpire threw his hat into the dirt and jammed a finger through the chain-link fence at Sarah, then watched Sarah press her face toward his and yell back. She'd make a hell of a coach, he thought. Team loyalty was job one.

When the little set-to ended, and the umpire's ruling stood, Sarah stomped back to her seat and the game progressed again. But as the pitcher wound up on the mound, one sound rose above all others in the crowd.

"Eh, batter, batter, batter, batter..."

Griffin sighed and waited for the pitch.

* * *

"You were great out there tonight, Griffin," Jack said as he chewed methodically on a wedge of pizza two hours later at Ferd Dante's Pizza Inferno. "That was some home run."

Griffin rubbed absently at the dirt stain streaking the right leg of his jeans from knee to thigh. He could already feel a bruise forming beneath.

"Yeah, the winning run, too," Sam added enthusiastically.

Griffin smiled at the two boys. "Well, I couldn't have done it without your mom's team spirit. She had me all fired up."

And not entirely because of her enthusiasm for the game, either, he thought. Every time the breeze had picked up and lifted her shirt to reveal a generous view of her smooth torso, he'd felt a rush of electricity spark through him like nobody's business. There was no doubt in his mind that's what had generated his final burst of energy. All that pent-up sexual awareness.

Sarah had the decency to blush sheepishly. "I, uh, I guess I should have warned you that I'm something of a sports fanatic," she said softly. "The boys' Little League coach has threatened to bar me from their games on more than one occasion. He doesn't think I take school sports in the spirit in which they're intended."

"Yeah, Mom's a fanatic, all right," Jack said. "Dad could never understand it. 'Course he would never even pitch to us, either, but we could always count on Mom."

Griffin couldn't help but wonder what kind of man would neglect the needs of his two children. Especially children who were as lovable and well adjusted as Sarah's clearly were.

"Hey, I've got no complaints about your mom's performance tonight," he told them. "It's been a long time since we've had a cheering section as enthusiastic as you three were." It had also been a long time since they'd won a game, he thought further. Tonight had been the first precinct's first win of the season. Griffin was fully willing to consider the two facts entirely related. He smiled at Sarah. "You must be a good-luck charm."

She smiled back, ready to reply, when the small group was interrupted by another group of people.

"Yo, there's the slugger!"

Stony clapped Griffin's right shoulder soundly, making him wince. Until that moment, Griffin hadn't realized he'd slid home on his arm, too. He was going to be a wreck tomorrow morning.

"Nice run tonight, Griffin," Elaine commented as she and Jonah joined Stony.

The three pulled up a vacant table near the others and sat down. Stony dropped a familiar arm around Elaine's shoulders and drew her close, a gesture that made Griffin's eyebrows arch in interest. Last he'd heard, Stony was washing his hands of the woman. But now his partner's behavior suggested the relationship was back on steady ground.

"Thanks, Elaine," he said, hoping his voice belied none of his curiosity.

She looked at Sarah then and added, "We saw Leonard at the bar as we came in. He was tossing back rattlesnakes. We asked him to join us, but when he heard you were going to be here, he declined and ordered another round."

"Leonard?" Sarah asked.

"The umpire," Griffin told her.

"Oh."

Stony chuckled. "I think what really got to him was when you suggested his mother had enjoyed a little fling with a blind fruit bat before he was born."

Sarah colored becomingly. "Well, that *was* a lousy call he made on Griffin. The ball was in bounds by a mile."

"Hey, you get no complaints from me," Stony told her. "But it may take Leonard a few days to recover from this game."

"Listen, Sarah," Elaine began again, "Jonah was wondering if Sam and Jack could spend the night at our place tonight. If it's all right with you, that is. I certainly don't mind."

"Yeah, Mom was the one to suggest it in the first place," Jonah told them. "I couldn't believe I didn't have to beg for a change."

Griffin wasn't sure which he noted first—Elaine's downcast eyes or Stony's puzzled expression as he watched her. But clearly there was something going on with his partner and Sarah's best friend, and he made a mental note to ask Stony about it at the next available moment.

"Uh, well," Elaine stammered, "I just thought, you know, that the boys might want to have a little more time together."

This time Stony was the one to look down, his gaze focused on a spot on the floor he nudged with his toe. "Look, I'd better get going," he said suddenly, pushing himself away from Elaine to stand. "I just remembered someplace I gotta be. See you later, Elaine. Bye, Jonah. Everybody."

And with that he left, weaving his way quickly through the crowd, until he'd disappeared from view. Griffin and Sarah exchanged bewildered looks, then turned their attention to Elaine, who still sat silently, as if Stony's behavior was nothing unusual.

"So what do you say?" she asked, her voice sounding unsteady and too bright. "Jack? Sam? You guys want to spend the night at our place?"

"Yeah!" the two boys answered in unison.

Sarah studied her friend for a moment, then reached quickly for her purse. She withdrew two dollars' worth of change and thrust the coins at her sons. "Here, guys. You and Jonah go play video games for a little while. Griffin?" she added pointedly. "You want to go with them?"

The three boys each snatched up a piece of pizza and their sodas and headed off for the game room. Griffin threw her a look that indicated he wasn't at all pleased to be dismissed along with the youngsters, but he said nothing. He only rose and picked up his beer and followed slowly in the direction the boys had disappeared. Sarah waited until they were all well away before turning to her friend again.

"Elaine? Is everything okay?"

Elaine's expression was inscrutable when her gaze met Sarah's. "Sure," she said simply. "Why wouldn't it be?"

"Well, because things seemed a little tense between you and Stony a minute ago. Then he stormed off for no reason. Kinda made me wonder if there was something wrong."

Elaine sighed deeply and shook her head. "Stony's just acting like a child because he wants something he can't have."

"And what's that?" Sarah asked.

"Me."

Sarah closed her eyes and opened them again slowly, only to see Elaine staring back at her with a level look. "What do you mean?" she asked.

"Just that Stony wants to get more . . . intimate . . . than I do right now."

"Oooh." Sarah nodded her understanding.

Elaine shoved a handful of hair restlessly over her shoulder and toyed with a pepperoni on the abandoned pizza. "Look, I thought inviting the boys to sleep over would keep Stony from trying to wrangle an invitation like that for himself. Earlier this evening, he suggested I send Jonah to your house for the night, and I told him that Jonah had already asked to have Jack and Sam over. I lied, all right? But I didn't know what else to say."

"Maybe you should just be honest with Stony," Sarah suggested. "Tell him how you feel."

"I can't."

"Why not?"

"Because I'm not sure how I feel."

Sarah opened her mouth to say something more, then snapped it shut again. For some reason, Elaine's dilemma sounded vaguely familiar, and for some reason, commenting on it right now made Sarah feel like a hypocrite.

"So you just thought it would be better to avoid the situation altogether," she concluded.

Elaine nodded, looking miserable. "And now he's mad at me."

"He'll get over it."

Elaine seemed to remember something then, because she turned to Sarah with a worried expression. "Hey, me having your kids over to my place isn't going to put *you* in a bind or anything, is it?"

"A bind?" Sarah asked, unsure what her friend meant.

"With Griffin, I mean."

"I don't follow you."

Elaine sat back in her chair and eyed her friend speculatively. "Well, I know you and Griffin aren't...you know. At least, I don't think you are. Are you?"

Sarah narrowed her eyes, puzzled. "Aren't...what?"

Elaine rolled her eyes in exasperation. "You know..." She made a gyrating motion with her hand to encourage her friend along.

Sarah shook her head.

Her friend uttered an impatient sound before fairly shouting, "Sleeping together!"

Now Sarah's eyes widened in shock. She threw two hasty glances left and right to make certain no one had heard her friend's outburst, before whispering loudly, "Of course not! Elaine! How could you even ask such a thing? He and I hardly know each other. Honestly."

Elaine smiled. "The way the two of you stare at each other all the time makes a person think you might know each other *very* well."

Sarah tilted her chin upward defensively. "What way?"

Elaine smiled. "Oh, like you can't wait to get home, tear each other's clothes off and cover each other with chocolate syrup. That way."

"Actually," Sarah began slowly, "it isn't so much chocolate syrup that preoccupies my thoughts as it is... handcuffs."

Elaine laughed. "I beg your pardon."

"Look, it's just a fantasy, okay? Lots of women fantasize about motorcycle cops and handcuffs and leather gloves. Happens all the time."

"I've never fantasized about that. My fantasies almost always involve food. Food and, on rare occasions, Nerf balls."

Sarah's brows arrowed downward at her friend's admission. "Yeah, well, I've read all about the handcuff thing. Nancy Friday says it's perfectly normal. And so does Dr. Ruth."

Elaine lifted the slice of pizza she'd nearly destroyed with her nervous fiddling and took a generous bite. "So you don't think there's any chance Griffin will put the make on you tonight?" she asked when she'd swallowed. "Now that the boys will be out of the way?"

"Well, I didn't say *that*...."

The two women looked at each other for a moment, then began to laugh.

"Look, I can handle Griffin Lawless," Sarah said as her chuckles subsided.

Elaine sighed. "You sure?"

She nodded. "Positive."

"Good. Because he's coming this way, and he doesn't look too happy."

Sarah pivoted quickly around to see Griffin approaching fast. She hadn't meant to dismiss him like a child when she'd asked—or rather told—him to join the boys. But thinking back on it now, she supposed that's exactly what she'd done. Naturally he'd be a little angry with her right now. Only for some reason, he seemed less angry than he did...intent. Just what that intention was, she could only wonder about right now. No doubt she'd find out soon enough, she thought.

The words she had just offered so carelessly to Elaine came back to haunt her. Could she indeed handle Griffin Lawless? she wondered. She was beginning to think such a feat was impossible. Unless "handling" him took on an entirely new, decidedly *literal* meaning. In which case, Sarah thought, she would probably be better off if she just stood up right now to face him—and ran away with all her might.

Six

Sarah's house was always so quiet when the boys were gone. Sometimes she found the break in the chaos a wonderfully relaxing change. Other times—like now—the silence rather unnerved her. Although, she conceded as she studied the man glowering at her from across the room, maybe her discomfort now was less a result of her children's absence than it was Griffin Lawless's presence.

He had scarcely spoken a half-dozen words to her since leaving Ferd Dante's Pizza Inferno a half hour ago. Elaine and Jonah had followed them home to collect Jack and Sam and their sleeping bags, but once that chattering group had left some moments ago, Sarah and Griffin had done little more than stare at each other. She supposed their sudden lack of communication should come as no surprise to her, considering the fact that the two of them had never been completely at ease when they were alone together. But for some reason, she felt as if the unsaid words hanging in the air between them tonight were much more important than what they usually didn't say to each other.

"I'm sorry," she finally said, hoping not only to get the conversation started, but also to bridge the gap that had formed between them. "I shouldn't have excluded you earlier tonight by sending you off after the boys. I was just worried about Elaine, and I didn't think she'd open up in front of you. You and Stony are such good friends, after all, and..." Her voice trailed off when she realized she wasn't sure how much she should reveal.

Griffin nodded, but said nothing.

Sarah tried not to be discouraged. "I don't blame you for being mad at me, but—"

"I'm not mad at you."

It was the longest string of words he'd offered her since she'd sent him away with the boys. She smiled, suddenly feeling encouraged. "Then why aren't you speaking to me?"

Griffin crossed the living room in a few easy strides, dropped his hands onto Sarah's shoulders and stared intently into her eyes. "Because ever since Elaine asked Jack and Sam over, ever since I realized I was going to have you to myself tonight, all I've been able to think about is..." He looked away briefly, drew in a deep breath and expelled it slowly. When he met Sarah's gaze again, he concluded unsteadily, "Is making love to you. And quite frankly, the thoughts I've been entertaining have left me a little speechless."

His bluntness startled her. She would have been lying if she said she hadn't been thinking about the same thing, but she certainly wasn't the kind of person who would come right out and announce it. She should have realized Griffin would be, though.

She opened her mouth to comment on his roughly uttered declaration, but all she was able to manage was "How about some coffee, hmm?"

He only continued to gaze at her, but she thought she detected a faint twitch at one corner of his mouth.

"Or...or a glass of wine?" she said, trying again. "I think that would be nice, don't you?"

"Sarah, I—"

She pulled quickly away from him and sped toward the kitchen, stepping up her speed when she felt Griffin following closely behind. She opened a cabinet by the sink and stretched up to rummage fitfully through its contents.

"Sarah," Griffin began again.

"I know I still have a nice bottle of something that I got for a Christmas present," she interrupted him as she pushed aside boxes of wild rice and cans of soup. "Something red. Elaine gave it to me, and she knows all about wine."

"Sarah."

"Her ex-husband owned a wine shop, you know."

"Sarah."

"I just need to remember where I—"

His arm suddenly appeared alongside the one she had thrust into the cabinet, corded with muscle and sprinkled with dark hair where her own was slender and smooth. He circled her wrist with strong fingers, but made no other move. Faced with such rigid differences in their physiques, Sarah felt something set to racing in her midsection. Griffin stood directly behind her, his body pressed intimately and without apology against hers.

Suddenly dizzy, she closed her eyes and inhaled deeply, only to find her lungs filled with the scent of him, a scent that was stark and masculine and utterly primal. Somehow she managed to continue with her search, his fingers curling around hers just as she located the wine she had been seeking. Together, they pulled the cool green bottle from its resting place and set it carefully on the counter.

Sarah began to reach up again, to retrieve two glasses from the top shelf, but Griffin's hand covered hers once more and halted her progress. Wordlessly she turned to face him, but dropped her gaze to the floor when she found it difficult to meet his eyes. Hesitantly he bent his head toward hers, and when she still did not look at him, brushed his lips against her temple. Instinctively she tilted her chin up toward the caress, and when she did, he touched his lips briefly to hers before pulling away. Then he repeated the gesture—another soft, quick brush of his lips on hers. Followed by another. Then another. And another.

Sarah flattened her hands against his chest, telling herself she should push him away. But beneath her fingers, she felt the warm, hard steel of his chest and the ever-quickening pulse of his heart, and found herself bunching the soft, faded fabric of his T-shirt in her fingers, pulling him even closer, instead. He wound an arm around her waist, then tangled his fingers in the curls at her nape. Finally, she did turn her face to his, and lost herself in the pale blue depths of his eyes.

For just a moment, she thought she saw a flicker of confusion in those eyes, thought she saw Griffin shake his head slowly in what appeared to be bewilderment or even denial. Then the look was gone, and he was kissing her again, this time with more insistence, this time with more aplomb.

She told herself she was crazy for letting him do it, called herself every kind of fool. Griffin Lawless was not the kind of man for her, not the kind who would want to settle down with a ready-made wife and family. She'd been so careful not to get involved with fly-by-night men since her divorce. In fact, she'd been careful not to get involved with any men at all. He was no different from the others, she tried to assure herself. There was no future in what they both obviously wanted to do tonight.

Then why did she want to do it so badly? she asked herself. She should want him to stop kissing her, should want to make sure things didn't go any further than they already had. But really, she had to admit when she felt the tip of his tongue touch the corner of her mouth, what she wanted to do was kiss him back.

So she did. With all the wanting, need and desire he exhibited himself. For long moments the couple remained locked in an embrace Sarah hoped would go on forever. She threaded her fingers through his hair, cupped his rough jaw in her palm and explored every solid inch of his arms, shoulders and back. Griffin, too, took time to investigate his discovery, lingering over every soft curve and smooth plane he encountered.

Suddenly, deftly, he switched their positions until he was the one leaning against the counter, then curved his hands possessively over her derriere to pull her into the cradle of his thighs. Sarah groaned, a wild little sound of surrender, and kissed him more deeply.

Griffin's head was spinning. He wasn't sure how it had happened, but he was on the verge of completely losing control. He knew what he was doing was crazy, knew he shouldn't have Sarah Greenleaf in his arms this way when he was investigating her brother for fraud. But he was a man who thrived on dangerous behavior, he reminded himself. And ever since meeting her, she had filled his head with thoughts of the most dangerous variety. He wanted her. Badly. And being with her now, like this, he could feel how badly she wanted him, too. So what was wrong with two people who wanted the same thing indulging in what each had to offer the other? They were consenting adults who clearly turned each other on. What was the harm in enjoying each other?

He felt her hands at his hips, clinging wildly to the belt loops of his jeans as if trying desperately to prevent her exploration of his body from venturing further. Knowing he'd be sorry for what he was about to do, Griffin covered her hand with his and loosed it from its grip, then placed her palm over the rigid crest that had risen under the zipper of his jeans.

Immediately her fingers took possession of him, and he groaned aloud at the exquisite shudder that wound through him at her touch. After that, all thoughts of the Wallace Greenleaf investigation fled, along with any doubts he might have had about making love to Sarah. As she raked her fingers slowly over him, he knew there was nothing that would stop him from doing what he had set out to do from the beginning—have his way with Sarah Greenleaf.

"Where's your bedroom?" he asked, wondering where he was finding the ability to speak coherently.

His question seemed to pull her out of the haze into which they had both apparently descended, but she met his gaze levelly with her own. "Through the dining room, at the end of the hall," she replied without hesitation.

Griffin nodded, then took her hand and led her in the direction she'd indicated. He found himself in a softly-lit room filled with old, feminine things—ornate Victorian furniture with flowery cushions, plants tumbling from antique pots, vintage botanical etchings and, tucked unobtrusively into the corner, a small bed draped with fine, delicate linens.

Suddenly he realized that while the rest of the house was a family dwelling furnished with the basic necessities and equipped to handle the roughhousing of two young boys, Sarah's bedroom was clearly her own exclusive haven. Somehow the knowledge that she had allowed him to penetrate the sanctity of her room humbled him a little, and he began to feel just the slightest touch of uncertainty about what they were planning to do.

But before he could question his concern further, Sarah came into his arms and kissed him, winding her arms around his neck, twining her fingers in his hair. And suddenly all his uncertainty fled. He dropped his hands to her waist, dipping below the cropped T-shirt for the first time to allow himself a sampling of the warm, soft skin beneath. He strummed her ribs as if playing a symphony upon them, then hesitated when he cradled her breast in the curve created by his thumb and index finger. With one gentle swipe upward, he caught her breast fully in his hand, smiling at the sound of Sarah's slight gasp.

"Oh, Griffin," she whispered unevenly.

The fingers in his hair gripped tighter, tipping his head toward hers. Instead of kissing him, however, she only pressed her forehead against his own and sighed deeply.

"It's been a long time for me," she said softly.

"Has it?" he said simply, aware the confession had been offered reluctantly.

She pulled her head away from his and nodded. "Not since . . . I mean, I've gone out with men since Michael, but I haven't . . . you know."

"You haven't been with anyone since your husband."

She shook her head and continued to avoid his gaze. "No. In fact, there was no one before Michael, either. I've only been with one man in my entire life. Pretty funny, huh?" she added with a nervous chuckle that afforded not a trace of amusement. "I, uh, I guess I'm not exactly the kind of woman you're used to dating."

Griffin curled a finger beneath her chin and turned her head until she was facing him fully, but her eyes remained downcast. Finally he said, "Hey."

Dark blond lashes lifted slowly, until he was gazing down into the seemingly endless depths of her brown eyes. For the first time he noted a few flecks of gold that shot out like sunbeams from her pupils.

"I'd like to think I'm not the kind of man you're used to dating, either. At least, I hope I'm not. I don't expect—or want—you to be like anyone other than yourself. If I wanted a different woman, I'd be with someone else right now. I want *you*, Sarah. And I can only hope you want me, too."

Sarah studied his face for a long time before replying. *Want* was actually a pretty tame word for what she was feeling for Griffin, she decided. But until she could come up with something to describe the galloping, frenzied heat that was burning her up inside, she supposed *want* would suffice.

"I don't understand what it is I feel for you, or why," she finally said, reaching for him again, "but I don't think I've ever wanted anything as much as I want you."

She watched as his lips curled into an easy, languorous smile. "Then take me, Sarah. I'm yours for the night."

She swallowed hard at his command, wondering what madness had come over her ever to think that she could handle the situation. *For the night*—that's how long he had said he was hers. The three little words bounced around in her head like a ceaseless echo. She tried not to dwell on the finite length of time those words indicated. Don't think about later, she told herself, dropping her hand to his belt buckle. For once in your life, just take something for yourself and revel in the moment.

Her eyes never left his as, with one gentle tug, she freed his belt from the buckle, then unfastened each of the buttons on his button-fly jeans. She stifled a groan when she realized he wasn't wearing any underwear, and focused instead on how to pull his T-shirt from the waistband. When her fingers stumbled over the task, Griffin reached behind himself to grab a fistful of the shirt, pulling it over his head with one quick gesture. He messed up his hair in the process, but Sarah had never seen a more glorious-looking man.

Every rigid muscle of his abdomen was clearly defined beneath a rich scattering of dark hair that covered his chest and torso and disappeared into his open jeans. Her hands were drawn like magnets to explore each tantalizing inch of him, and she marveled at the contradictions of soft skin and hard sinew, of coarse hair that sprang to life beneath her fingertips. Her fingers lingered at the pink, puckered skin on his shoulder, a quick bolt of fear shimmying down her spine as she realized how close she had come never to having this man in her life. She pressed her lips briefly against the scar, then ventured lower in her explorations.

As she took her time becoming familiar with him, Griffin seemed to grow impatient. After dropping his hands to unfasten her cutoffs, he caught the hem of her T-shirt and pulled it up over her head. Before she realized what was happening, Sarah was standing flush and half-naked against him, an infinitely more intimate touch than anything she could have anticipated.

"You know, that bed of yours seems awfully small," Griffin said suddenly. Only then did she realize his attention had been drawn to something beyond the agitated state of arousal that had risen between them.

Before she could answer, he pushed his hands down past her waist, under the waistband of her jeans and beneath her panties, cupping the bare flesh of her fanny fully in his warm palms. All she was able to manage for a moment was a softly uttered, "Oh." Then Griffin began to walk toward the bed, leaving Sarah no alternative but to walk backward with him, clutching his big biceps to keep herself from stumbling. As they moved, his hands continued to stroke the soft contours of her derriere, but what caught her attention even more was the rigid swell of him pressing against her belly.

"Yeah, it's a small bed all right," Griffin went on as he came to a halt beside the piece of furniture in question. "I guess we're just going to have to stay real close to each other."

He kissed her as he tumbled her to the bed, shucking her cut offs and panties as they fell. Always fair-minded, Sarah pushed insistently at his jeans until they, too, lay in a heap on the floor, then struggled to turn down the bed—no easy feat amid their squirming bodies. The shedding of those final garments was the abandonment of what few apprehensions either may have had left, and they came to each other with urgent need.

Her senses caught fire at each place Griffin touched. He seemed to be everywhere at once, his lips nibbling hers while his fingers toyed with her breasts and explored parts of her she barely knew herself. The soft bristles of his mustache introduced an entirely new realm of sensual experience, and more than once she found herself giggling with ticklish delight. But as his ministrations became more insistent and extravagant, her laughter eventually faded.

When he rolled her onto her back and rose above her, Sarah suddenly panicked. She remembered vaguely that there were often repercussions of the sexual act that came about later—two of those repercussions happened to be spending the night with their best friend tonight. She tried hastily to calculate the days that had passed since her last period, but discovered quickly that in the state she was in now, she was scarcely familiar with her own name, let alone the biological comings and goings of her reproductive system.

She faltered when Griffin began to kiss her neck and skim his fingers along the inside of her thigh to encourage her legs apart. Oh, who cares? she thought briefly. But on the heels of that thought came another, that of a bouncing baby girl with black hair and blue eyes identical to her father's—a father who was nowhere to be found in the picture.

"Wait!" she cried.

Griffin lifted his head from between her breasts and gazed down at her through narrowed eyes. "Wait?" he repeated. "May I ask for what?"

Sarah smiled at his expression, loving him for it. She knew if she called it quits right now, he'd abide by her wishes. He wouldn't much like it, but he'd go along with her. She touched her finger to his lips, realizing there was more truth to her reaction than she had first thought. She did love him for it. She was beginning to understand that she loved him for a lot of reasons. When it had happened or how, she wasn't sure. But somehow she had let herself fall flat on her face in love with Griffin Lawless.

She removed her finger and raised her lips to his for a quick kiss. "I, uh, I just remembered that there's every possibility I could wind up pregnant for this."

His eyes widened in surprise, as if he, too, had forgotten just how babies came into the world. "Oh, yeah. I don't suppose you, uh, you know... have something."

"Well, I'm sure I still have a diaphragm around here somewhere. But there are necessary, ah, *accessories,* shall we say, that go with it, and I don't have any of those right now. And a diaphragm isn't guaranteed effective without them."

Griffin nodded. "Well, don't take this the wrong way, but... I do sort of carry some protection with me all the time—in my wallet, no less."

Sarah laughed. "How could I take that the wrong way? You forget you're talking to a woman who carries a condom around in her glove compartment."

"Yeah, without even realizing it."

"Griffin?"

"Yeah?"

"Shut up and get moving. Or do you want me to go through your pants for you?"

He grinned as he pushed himself away from her. "Seems to me you've already done that once, and look where it got us."

"Well, hurry up so we can get back there again."

He did, and they were. Seemingly without missing a beat, Sarah found herself back in his arms, with her fingers buried in his hair and his lips wreaking havoc on her senses. And then suddenly, without warning, he was inside her, pushing himself deeper and deeper until completely sheathed in the delicate contours of her body. She cried out, marveling at the strength of him springing to life. He pulled away from her for only a moment, then plummeted inside again. Almost of their own free will, her legs circled his waist, and she matched his rhythm in a sensual dance as old as nature.

Together they climbed higher, sensations multiplying all along the way. Just when Sarah thought she could no longer tolerate the exquisite fire burning through her, Griffin drove her further, taking them to a place that nearly sent them both over the edge. Yet before she could let herself go, she felt the tension inside her build again, until she nearly went mad demanding satisfaction. With one final burst of energy, they went spiraling out of control, clinging to each other lest they become lost forever. For several long moments, they continued to cling to each other, their hearts pounding in unified rhythm, their breath commingling as it stirred the air around them.

"Wow," Sarah said when she was able to manage speech again. "That was amazing."

Griffin nodded, but said nothing. He buried his head in the damp, fragrant hollow where her neck and shoulder joined, placing a kiss on her salty skin. Something inside him had snapped at some point while he was making love to Sarah, and he still hadn't quite come to terms with what it was. He didn't want to think about it, didn't want to wonder what it meant. So instead he tried to do what he always did after he'd just made love to a woman. He tried not to let it get to him.

But to no avail. For some reason, this time it had gotten to him good. Sarah Greenleaf was inside him now, in some deep place that he hadn't known existed until this moment. He lifted his head and gazed down at her, shaking his head at the expression on her face and the look in her eyes. Whatever was happening between them hadn't affected him alone, he thought. He smiled at her, but for some reason the smile felt false. So he lifted a hand to brush away the damp curls clinging to her forehead, and pressed his lips to her temple.

"Griffin?"

"Shh."

He would think about it in the morning, he thought, pulling the covers up over them and nestling in beside Sarah. Wordlessly he turned her so that her back was against his front, draping a strong arm around her waist, pulling her close.

Tomorrow, he thought again. Surely by then, everything would make sense.

Sarah awoke slowly, not quite sure where she was at first. The early-morning sun slanting through the bedroom window felt warm on her bare back, and she wondered vaguely what had happened to the pajamas she usually wore. Her antique sleigh bed—larger than a single but smaller than a double—felt different somehow, more...intimate...than usual. She stretched her arm across the mattress and clenched a fistful of sheet in her fingers, murmuring in delight at the pleasant sensations wandering through her body.

What a magnificent dream she'd had. All night long, her brain had played host to wondrous images—scenes of her body tangled up with Griffin Lawless's in a most intriguing sexual encounter. She sighed deeply, marveling at how his scent seemed to cling to the pillow and how even the sheets felt warm from his body. It was amazing, she thought blissfully, how some dreams seemed so real.

Hearing the sound of the shower switch on in the next room, Sarah snapped her eyes open. That had been no dream, she recalled suddenly. All those erotic visions she'd been playing back in her brain were in fact her memories of the night before. She groaned as she rolled over onto her back, dropping her arm over her eyes. She was lying naked in her bed amid a virtual war zone of messed-up sheets, and Griffin Lawless was in the adjoining bathroom, taking a shower after having done things to her that had made her feel more exquisite than she could ever have imagined feeling.

What have I done? Sarah asked herself wildly. How had this happened? The answers to those questions came readily enough. She'd finally allowed herself to completely cut loose with a man who had her tied up in knots, and it had happened because she fancied herself in love with him.

"Oh, boy," she muttered to no one in particular.

She lifted her arm away from her face and stared at the ceiling. She told herself she should feel guilty, tried to berate herself for having done something so stupid. Unfortunately, try as she might to regret what had happened, Sarah could only smile, instead. She wasn't some starry-eyed teenager the morning after the prom worrying about what would happen next. She was a mature adult, a grown woman capable of raising two kids and running a business, a woman who was realistic about the future and knew how to take responsibility for her actions.

She wondered what Griffin would like for breakfast.

It was Sunday, she remembered, and the shop was closed. How convenient. Surely Griffin didn't have to work on Sunday. They could spend the whole day together. Maybe they could stop by Elaine's and pick up the boys and head to the park for a picnic. Or the four of them could go to a movie. And then Griffin could stay for dinner. Of course, it would be nice if he could stay the night again, too, but with the boys home, that would be impossible. Still, there would be other opportunities for the two of them to be alone together.

For the first time in a long time, Sarah was actually excited about what the day ahead held for her. Moving quickly, she rolled out of bed, grabbed a pair of khaki shorts and an oversize red T-shirt from her dresser and headed for the hall bathroom to wash her face and get dressed. She had just switched on the coffeemaker and was about to inspect the contents of her refrigerator, when a series of loud raps shook the back door.

Who could possibly be dropping by unannounced at eight a.m. on a Sunday? she wondered. Before she even opened the door, she knew.

"Wally," she greeted the man who stood on her back porch. He was dressed in his golf clothes—lime green slacks and a canary yellow polo shirt, with a red-and-purple plaid driver's cap poised precariously on the back of his head. She squinted at the color combination, placing a hand over her eyes to shield them. "It's a little early, don't you think?"

He ignored her comment, kissing her briefly on the cheek as he pushed past her. "Great, you're making coffee. I've only had two cups this morning and can barely see straight."

Instead of closing the door behind him, Sarah left it open, standing pointedly beside it with her hands on her hips, glaring at her brother.

"What?" he asked.

She shook her head in disbelief. "Has it ever occurred to you that it might be nice to call before you drop by? Or better yet, not to come by at all until you're invited?"

He made a face at her. "Sarah," he said. His tone of dismissal put her teeth on edge. "It's me—Wally. I'm your brother, remember? We don't have to stand on ceremony."

With a dry smile, she replied, "Oh, come on, Wally. Sure we do."

He waved his hand at her as if she'd just made a wonderful joke. "Frankly, though, I'm surprised to find you up and at 'em this time of morning. I figured you'd still be in bed."

Sarah gave in, closed the back door and went to the cupboard for two mugs. Wally would find out soon enough why she was up this early, she thought with a smile. Neither of the cups she held was for him.

"Then why did you stop by?" she asked. "Obviously you weren't too concerned about waking me up."

"I got a letter from Mom yesterday, and she figured she'd save on postage by sticking one for you in the same envelope." He reached into his back pocket and extracted the missive in question.

"A woman who would invest good money in a topless cafeteria suddenly wants to save twenty-nine cents by doubling up on her mail," Sarah muttered as she took the letter from him.

"You know Mom."

"Yeah, I do."

She was about to comment further, but the appearance of Griffin at the door connecting her kitchen to her dining room stopped her. He wore only his jeans from the day before. His hair was still damp from the shower, but he had run a comb through the thick, unruly tresses. Tiny droplets of water clung to the hair on his chest, winking in the light like miniature diamonds, taunting her until they disappeared beneath the waistband of his jeans. Muscles roped and corded his arms and chest, and she couldn't help the sigh that erupted from somewhere deep inside her soul. Good heavens, had she really made love with such a man the night before?

"Sarah, I—"

His words halted abruptly when he saw Wally. Sarah held her breath as the two men evaluated each other. Almost as if daring Wally to say something, Griffin raised his arms to brace them against the doorjamb, leaning forward in a way she could only call menacing. Wally's only concession to Griffin's defiant stance was to straighten in his chair and uncross his legs. For long moments, no one spoke. Griffin eyed Wally. Wally eyed Griffin. And Sarah eyed them both.

"Uh, Griffin," she finally said, breaking up what she feared would be a never-ending silence, "this is my brother, Wally. Wally Greenleaf."

Griffin's posture changed immediately. She didn't know why, but for some reason, she was certain he became uncomfortable when he discovered who the intruder was. More than uncomfortable, she amended when she noted the way his eyes flashed at the other man. Almost hostile. How odd.

She supposed his reaction was only normal. What man would want his first meeting with a woman's family to occur immediately following what had clearly been a night of lovemaking? Still, it wasn't as though she was some blushing virgin. She'd been married, after all, and had two children. It was no secret that she must already know *something* about the sexual act. And late twentieth century morality did not dictate that a brother had to fight for his sister's honor. Nowadays a brother's sister was perfectly capable of fighting for herself. Usually.

"And, Wally," she continued quickly, "this is Griffin Lawless. My, uh . . ."

Well, now, that was a tricky one, she thought. Just what exactly was Griffin in the scheme of things? Calling him her "boyfriend" seemed a little silly, since he was clearly, in no way, a boy. "Lover" was too presumptuous—although she was fast falling in love with Griffin, she wasn't certain how he felt about her yet. "Significant other" was too trendy, while "beau" was too old-fashioned. "Hunka hunka burnin' love" was the phrase that came most readily to Sarah's mind, but that was probably more than Wally needed to know. Yet she had better come up with something before her brother took it upon himself to draw his own conclusions and think Griffin was just some guy she'd picked up in a bar the night before.

"My, uh . . ." she said, trying again.

"I'm a friend of Sarah's," Griffin answered for her, stepping into the kitchen to offer his hand to Wally.

There was a wariness about the gesture that Sarah couldn't ignore, but she didn't dwell on it, because she was too busy fretting about Griffin's classification of himself. He'd called himself her friend. Was that all he considered himself to be? Did most friends do what the two of them had done the night before? Sarah had never done it with any of her friends. She hadn't even *thought* about doing that with her friends. But maybe Griffin did. Maybe what happened last night was nothing new for him at all. Maybe all his women friends wound up in his bed. Or he wound up in theirs. Or . . .

She sighed fitfully, trying to push the thought away. Men were supposed to be the ones who hated the phrase "Let's be friends," she reminded herself. Women were bigger than that, weren't they? At the moment, she wasn't sure.

Wally stood as he shook hands, but seemed no more amiable about doing so than Griffin appeared to be. Sarah didn't know what was going on. Some guy thing dictated by the laws of the animal kingdom, she supposed. Brother looks out for sister while predator licks his chops, or some such thing.

"So, Wally, won't you stay for breakfast?" she asked sweetly, already knowing the answer.

"Uh, no. No, thanks. I'm meeting Jerry for breakfast at the club." He glanced down at his watch. "In fact, I'm running late as it is."

"Don't rush off on my account," Griffin said. But his smile suggested he wished Wally would rush off—right off a bridge at high speed.

"Thanks, but I really should get going. Sarah," he added as he kissed his sister goodbye and hurried out the back door, "I'll see you soon."

"No doubt," she said as the door slammed shut behind him.

She turned to smile at Griffin, but her smile quickly fell. His expression was anything but happy. In fact, he looked as if he wanted to hit something. Hard.

"Coffee?" she asked, the question ending in a near squeak.

He nodded once. "Please."

Griffin watched Sarah's movements closely, wondering if she could detect the tremors of anger spiraling through his body. He wasn't angry at her. Hell, he wasn't even angry at her brother, if truth be told. He was angry at himself. Angry that he'd conveniently chosen to forget that the woman he'd spent the night making love to was the sister of a man he was investigating, a man he was *this close* to putting behind bars for a good stretch.

She turned wordlessly and handed him his coffee, remembering that he took it black. Griffin sipped it slowly, stalling as long as he could before talking to her, wondering how he had managed to botch something up so thoroughly.

When he had awakened that morning to find Sarah nestled beside him, he had been nearly overcome by how utterly right the position had felt. She had been curled against him with her head tucked into the hollow of his chin, the fingers of one hand curled into a loose fist against his chest, while the other hand cupped his hip. His arms had been looped around her waist, the one she was lying on numb due to a lack of circulation. He hadn't minded a bit, though. She had been warm and soft and redolent with the lingering aroma of the lovemaking they had shared, and Griffin had wanted nothing more than to wake her up and start all over again.

He should be able to awaken in such a way every morning, he thought. Memories of the way in which they had turned to each other time and time again during the night nearly knocked the breath right out of him. They had responded to each other as if they were two halves of one whole, a unified body that had been separated for far too long. He had wanted to join them together again. But quite frankly, he hadn't thought he'd be able to manage it just yet.

So he had placed a quiet kiss on her forehead and disengaged himself as easily as he could to slip off to the shower. He had halfway hoped she would remain asleep for most of the morning, just so he could come out and watch her for a while. But when he'd emerged from the bathroom, she'd been gone. Now she stood before him, looking soft and rumpled and confused, and all the anger that had welled up inside him at Wallace Greenleaf's surprising appearance gradually began to fade.

But it didn't go away completely.

"What would you like for breakfast?" she asked then.

Griffin tensed. It was her tone of voice more than the question itself that disturbed him. The question implied her certainty that he would be staying for breakfast, and he wasn't quite sure how he should interpret that. But her voice, so matter-of-fact sounding when he felt so confused inside... That was what put him on edge. Part of him—a *big* part of him—wanted to spend the rest of the day with Sarah and her family, doing all the things that families normally did together on Sunday. And he could see clearly that such a pursuit was exactly what Sarah had on her mind, too.

But another part of him knew it would be a big mistake to let this thing between them go any further than it already had as long as he was tied up with the investigation of her brother. It wasn't ethical, it wasn't moral and it sure as hell wasn't nice. But then he noted the way Sarah was looking at him, noted the way her thin T-shirt draped lovingly over the swell of her breasts, remembered that one wild sound she had made just before she'd lost herself to her passion, and his conviction began to waver.

"Coffee," he forced himself to say before his thoughts could race beyond his control. "Just coffee is fine. I can't stay."

Her expression fell at his announcement. "You're leaving?"

He made himself nod in the affirmative, even though he wanted more than anything to reply in the negative. "There's a case I need to work on today."

"What kind of case?"

She would ask, Griffin thought. He sipped his coffee again to stall. "I really can't talk about it. The guy we're investigating doesn't know it." Yet, he added to himself. But any day now...

"Oh."

The one-syllable reply was almost Griffin's undoing. That single, tiny sound had the effect of a bazooka shot off right beside his ear. He heard disappointment, uncertainty, regret and not a little fear all tied up in that simple, softly uttered interjection.

"Sarah," he began, trying to think of some way to explain.

"No, that's all right," she assured him. "I understand. I should have realized. You must be very busy."

He inhaled a restless breath and expelled it slowly, wishing he could think of something that would allay her concern, but completely at a loss as to how he could explain without revealing the nature of his investigation. "I'm sorry," he said, instead.

She arched her brows in resignation. "Yeah, me, too."

"Look, Sarah, I—"

But she cut him off. "It's okay, really."

She lifted one shoulder in what he supposed was meant to be a careless shrug, but it missed the mark by a mile. Any fool could see that she was hurting inside. And seeing as how he was probably the biggest fool of all, Griffin couldn't miss the reaction. She thought he was abandoning her. Thought he was the kind of man who would sleep with a woman, then desert her the following morning. Then again, he supposed, in a way she was right. Because as things stood now, he couldn't allow what had happened last night to happen again.

Sarah was wrong, he thought. It wasn't okay at all. He'd managed to muck things up royally. But he'd make it up to her, he promised himself. Then immediately, he saw the irony in that. Just when was he likely to make it up to her? As long as he was investigating her brother without her knowing about it, he was effectively lying to her. Some foundation for a relationship. So maybe he could make it up to her after the investigation was concluded, when he'd been responsible for putting her brother behind bars. Oh, yeah. No doubt Sarah would be really happy to cozy up to him then.

"Look, I really should get going," he said suddenly. "Thanks for the coffee."

Sarah nodded mutely, but didn't meet his gaze. More than ever before, Griffin wished he knew the right thing to say to put things back the way they were before. Before he had gone and fallen halfway in love.

"I'll call you," he said.

"Sure you will." She stood stoically with her arms crossed over her abdomen, giving him the impression that she was trying to hold herself together. Still she refused to look at him.

He placed his coffee cup on the counter and took a step toward her, then curled his fingers firmly around her nape. When she didn't respond, he rubbed his thumb softly up the column of her throat, then followed the line of her jaw.

Sarah stirred a little, shifting her weight from one foot to the other. He felt her pulse quicken beneath his fingertips and felt a little better. Bending forward, he pressed his lips to her temple for just a moment before pulling away.

"I'll call you," he repeated.

Sarah nodded again, lifting her head to finally stare into his eyes. "You'd better."

Griffin managed to lift one corner of his mouth in a smile before releasing her. He allowed himself the luxury of tangling his fingers one last time in the silky curls at her nape, then turned to collect his things from the bedroom. He still wasn't sure how he was going to work this situation out, still didn't know what the hell he was going to do about Wallace or Sarah Greenleaf. But one thing was certain. He wasn't going to let either of them get away.

Seven

"Thanks for the coffee," Sarah mimicked angrily to herself as she watched the door close softly behind Griffin. "It was the least I could do!" she called out after him, knowing he couldn't hear her. "You creep!"

Sure, he was going to call her. She'd heard that one before. Maybe she hadn't dated extensively since her divorce—or before her marriage come to think of it—but every woman in her right mind knew what the phrase "I'll call you" meant. It was the big brush-off, pure and simple.

How could he do that to her after the night they'd spent together? she asked herself. Hey, she was a realist—she hadn't been expecting miracles this morning, that she'd wake to hear him murmuring his undying devotion to her and swearing he couldn't live without her. But she'd assumed he would at least stay for breakfast. She glanced over at the still-steaming, half-full cup of coffee on the counter. Breakfast, she repeated to herself with a rueful shake of her head. He hadn't even finished his coffee.

She jumped when the phone jangled behind her, and for one brief moment, a flicker of hope ignited in her heart. Then she realized that unless Griffin had a cellular phone on his motorcycle, it probably wasn't going to be him at the other end of the line.

"It's Elaine," her friend said in response to Sarah's greeting. "Are you up yet?"

She sighed. "I'm up."

"What's wrong? You don't sound so good."

Sarah wondered how much she should tell Elaine, then decided she wasn't in the mood to discuss anything about Griffin Lawless right now. "Nothing. I'm just not awake yet."

"Do you, uh, have any...oh, plans for the day?" Elaine asked further, clearly fishing for information.

I wish, Sarah thought. "No, no plans."

"Oh. Sorry."

"It's no big deal," she lied. "Griffin said he had to work on some case. Have you heard from Stony?"

"No, but it's still pretty early in the morning for him to be up and alert enough to figure out the phone. Not to mention that our parting last night might keep him quiet for a while yet."

"Maybe he's working, too."

"No," Elaine replied quickly. "He said something yesterday about he and I taking Jonah to the Natural History Museum, but we never finalized anything."

"But he's Griffin's partner, isn't he?" Sarah asked.

"Yes."

"So if Griffin had to work on a case, wouldn't Stony be working with him?"

Elaine's hesitation before replying told Sarah more than she really wanted to know. "Well, not necessarily," her friend said in that tone of voice women use when trying to let each other down as easily as possible. "Just what exactly happened between the two of you last night?"

"Something that shouldn't have," Sarah replied reluctantly.

"Oh."

Fearful her friend might launch into some tea-and-sympathy routine, Sarah continued hastily, "Maybe we could take the boys to a movie or something."

Elaine hesitated before replying, and Sarah held her breath, willing her friend not to pursue the topic of last night. Elaine seemed to get the message, however, because she said, "There's a movie called *Firestorm* they want to see. I read the review in this morning's paper. It's loaded with high-tech weaponry, lots of explosions, bloody dismemberments, the foulest language known to man and women with big hooters."

"I think the Hanlon Theater is showing a Disney double feature," Sarah remembered. "*Old Yeller* and *Davy Crockett*."

"The boys will hate it."

"So what are we waiting for?"

"I'll pick you up at noon. We can eat lunch first."

Sarah hung up the phone feeling a little better than she had after Griffin's sudden departure. She and Elaine were *not* taking their frustration with the adult male population out on their sons, she assured herself. But wasn't it nice to know that there were still *some* males in the world over whom women had control. At least until they were grown-ups, she amended as she went to take a shower. At which point their mothers generally turned them loose to bother someone else.

At six p.m. two Mondays later, Griffin sat in the living room of his apartment, sipping a beer and thinking about Sarah. Or, more specifically, about making love to Sarah. Or, even more specifically, about the way Sarah's skin had tasted and smelled when he'd touched his tongue to her—

With a heartfelt groan, he jumped up from his seat, upsetting the coffee table and bashing his knee in the process.

When he instinctively jerked down to cradle his injured joint, his beer bottle went flying, spilling a wide amber wake across the hardwood floor before splitting clean in two. He swore colorfully, hobbled to the kitchen for a towel and thought about Sarah some more.

More than two weeks had passed since he'd seen her, and he hadn't called her once. But he'd wanted to. Not a day had gone by that he hadn't reached for the phone to punch the numbers that would connect him to her. Even stronger had been his desire to stop by the judge's house while she was working there. Or rather, *his* house, Griffin amended uncomfortably, still unused to his ownership of the Mercer home. He remembered how she had looked the day he'd surprised her there, the way her wet T-shirt had clung to her body and how her damp curls had fastened to her forehead.

But inevitably, such a reminder also roused memories of how Sarah had looked after the two of them had made love, something he just shouldn't have allowed to happen. Yet.

The investigation into the illegal doings of Wallace Greenleaf was really heating up. He and Stony were only days away from being able to petition for a search warrant, and once that happened, Wally and his sidekick, Jerry, would be history. Their little cheat-the-public and money-for-political-favors machines would be effectively and permanently shut down.

Griffin couldn't help but wonder how much Sarah knew about her brother's professional life. He got the impression that although the two siblings saw each other from time to time and spoke civilly, even affectionately, to each other, they weren't particularly close. Not in the sense that they shared a good portion of their lives with each other. And Wally Greenleaf didn't exactly seem the type of man who would let his sister in on his shady dealings. Nor did Sarah seem the type of woman who would stand by and let her brother get away with cheating people.

No, Griffin was sure she had no idea what Wally and his partner were up to. And what they were up to was bribing public officials and bilking gullible citizens out of their life savings. It left a bad taste in Griffin's mouth to realize there were people in the world capable of taking advantage of others in such a way.

What Wally Greenleaf and Jerry Schmidt did was convince unsuspecting people—usually the elderly or those who were struggling to build even the tiniest of nest eggs and desperate for fast cash—to invest every nickel they had in some scheme the two owners of Jerwal, Inc., had no intention of following through on. They pretended to invest the money in hiring and contracting, then bribed some local government figure to block the project with a lot of legal hoo-ha. And then all that was left was to tell the investors that their money was gone, their investment a bust, thanks to a lot of legal and political tangles that no one could have possibly foreseen. So sorry about that, but maybe they'd be interested in another project Jerwal had going.

Griffin wiped up the last of his spilled beer and carried the broken pieces of bottle to the kitchen. He felt edgy and anxious, trying to think of some way to work off his tension.

Immediately he remembered a terrific way to work off tension—diving deeply into Sarah while she cried out her demands with a ragged desperation that rivaled his own. As quickly as the graphic image entered his mind, he pushed it away. There was little chance she wanted to see him right now. Not after the way they'd parted two weeks ago, with his telling her he'd call her and never following through.

Dammit, why did this have to be so complicated? he wondered, lifting a hand to rub at the knot forming on the back of his neck. He suddenly felt the need to get out of his apartment for a little while. He would go nuts sitting here thinking about Sarah all night. He grabbed his helmet from the top of the refrigerator and headed out the back door.

Maybe he couldn't release his tension making love to Sarah, he thought, but a man had other alternatives.

Sarah looked through the passenger-side window at the big, marble, romanesque building that housed the first precinct. The place was quiet, not surprising for a Monday night, but a few people came and went through the heavy doors, some in uniform, some in plainclothes. None of them was Griffin, though, she realized, then immediately chastised herself for even bothering to look for him.

She sighed impatiently before asking, "Elaine, why did you bring me here?"

"I didn't bring *you* here, I brought *me* here. I have some stuff I promised I'd drop off for Stony."

"Can we go in, too?" Jonah asked from the back seat. He turned to Jack and Sam. "I've been in the police station before," he announced proudly, his voice suggesting that his presence was the result of a number of felony offenses. "Lots of times."

Elaine rolled her eyes and gazed at her son in the rearview mirror. "Twice," she corrected him. "And neither time because you were in trouble. Only because we were meeting Stony."

Jonah frowned at his mother, feeling what Sarah supposed was his disappointment that Elaine had ruined what would have been a beautiful story of an eight-year-old's lawlessness and adventure.

"And no, you may not come inside," Elaine added. "I don't want to be here all night. It'll be past your bedtimes before long."

"Aw, Mom..."

"Aw, Mrs. Bingham..."

The complaints were offered in a petulant, off-key chorus, and Elaine turned to Sarah in a silent plea for help. Sarah shook her head in defeat. "Oh, let them go in. I'll keep an eye on them while you look for Stony."

"You have no idea what you're getting yourself into," Elaine cautioned.

"Hey, I've got *two* of them," Sarah countered. "I know *exactly* what I'm getting myself into."

All five exited the car at the same time, but the boys were well into the squad room before the women caught up with them. Jonah took a seat atop Stony's desk and concentrated on balancing a pen on his index finger, while Jack and Sam inspected a bulletin board full of wanted posters, trying to discern whether they knew any of the men portrayed in the grainy black-and-white photos. Jack was certain one was Mr. Pike, the gym teacher at their school, but Stony managed to reassure him otherwise.

Sarah couldn't help but smile at the scene, curious about her friend's misgivings where Stony was concerned. He was clearly a man who loved children, and by the expression in his eye when he looked at her, was also clearly devoted to Elaine. Sarah wondered if Griffin would be as patient with the boys, then remembered how attentive he had been at her house the night he'd come over for dinner. Griffin, too, would make a good father. Jack and Sam adored him, and he appeared to be a natural with the boys. Too bad he didn't seem to show the same interest in their mother, she thought morosely, recalling for the thousandth time that he hadn't called her as he'd promised.

"Griff's in the exercise room," she heard Stony say, and she realized he and Elaine had been speaking for some moments while she'd been lost in thought.

"What?" she asked, turning to Stony, although she had understood his statement perfectly well.

He smiled, and Sarah could have sworn there was a somewhat devilish quality about it. He pointed toward the other side of the room.

"Through those double doors, down the stairs at the end of the hall, first door on your left."

It rather annoyed Sarah the way her heart took off at the realization that Griffin was in the same building. What dif-

ference did it make? she asked herself. He had no desire to
see her, or he would have called. Whether or not he was in
the building was immaterial. She would not go looking for
him when he obviously did not wish to be found by her.

She met Stony's gaze and shrugged. "So next time you see
him, tell him I said hi."

"Why don't you run down and tell him yourself?" he
asked. There was an underlying challenge in his voice.

Sarah lifted her chin defensively, never one to back down
from a dare. "All right," she said. "I will."

And with that, she spun on her heel and headed in the direction Stony had indicated. When she first entered the exercise room, she thought it was empty. The equipment
looked bleak and skeletal with no one using it, and garish
fluorescent light tinged everything with an odd, vaguely blue
tint that threw harsh black shadows everywhere. The silence was deafening. She was about to turn around and
leave, when she heard something, a hollow, irregular *thump,
thump . . . thump-thump.* Seeing a door on the other side of
the room, she made her way to it and discovered it led into
a gymnasium. And on the other side of the gym, she saw
Griffin. Looking very angry.

He was barefoot, wearing only a pair of ragged gray
sweatpants and well-worn boxing gloves. He pounded his
fists brutally against the leather punching bag, perspiration
streaming down his face and chest. When she noted his teeth
were clamped down hard on a smoldering cigar, Sarah
smiled. Some workout.

She pushed through the door silently and leaned against
the wall, watching him. His footwork was impressive. He
feinted and danced gracefully before heaving his fists into
the bag of sand. The bag swayed backward, the chain holding it jangling a bit, then swayed forward to be hit again.
Griffin slugged it five or six times in quick succession, then
skipped backward before lunging forward once more.

Sarah found the movements fascinating. Muscles bunched
and rippled in his arms and abdomen every time he came

forward, then relaxed when he moved away. And each time his fist made contact with the bag, he made a sound—not quite a groan, not quite a cry—but something primal and masculine and utterly arousing.

She must have made some sound in reply, because suddenly Griffin glanced up and saw her. Immediately he began to move toward her, his motions fluid, deft and confident, making Sarah feel like some small, defenseless prey. In a matter of seconds he stood before her. His black hair was wet with perspiration, falling forward, clinging to his forehead. His blue eyes seemed deeper than usual somehow, bright with exhilaration at the flow of blood that must be zinging through his system.

She watched, fascinated, as a trickle of sweat rolled down his cheek, curved past his jaw and down his throat, winding over his chest to disappear in the dark hair that spiraled down his abdomen. She wanted to follow that route with her tongue, to taste the life she felt pulsing from him, to lose herself completely in Griffin Lawless. Helplessly she closed her eyes and inhaled deeply, growing dizzy from the scent of him and at having him so close again. When she opened her eyes, he was still there, studying her with a maddening intensity and any number of unasked questions. She stood silently, not certain how she should answer them.

He shifted to rest his weight on one foot, his gloved hands settled on his hips and his cigar jutting from the corner of his mouth, but he didn't speak right away. For long moments they only stared at each other, and Sarah wished with all her heart that she knew what he was thinking.

Finally he asked, "What are you doing here?"

"Looking for you," she replied without thinking. She hurried to clarify, "I mean, I'm here with Elaine and the boys. She had to drop something off for Stony."

Griffin shrugged, ignoring the last part of her statement when he said simply, "So you found me."

"So I did."

When she didn't elaborate, he reached for his cigar, surprisingly adept at removing it from his mouth, considering he still wore his boxing gloves. "What is it you want, Sarah?"

He emphasized the word *want* as if it promised satisfaction to every desire she would ever have. Her mouth suddenly felt dry, and she licked her lips in an effort to ease the sensation. She noted that her action caught his attention and held it, and her heart trip-hammered against her rib cage at the lascivious thoughts burning up her brain.

"You never called me," she said.

He frowned. "I know, and I'm sorry. I've been working on a—"

"A case," she finished for him. "I know. A difficult case. A case I would think Stony would be working on with you."

"He is."

"But Stony isn't working right now," she said. "And neither are you."

"I know, but—"

Before she realized what she was doing, Sarah took Griffin's gloved hand in hers, removed the cigar and threw it on the floor, stamping her foot on it to put it out. Then she unlaced his glove and jerked it clumsily from his hand, tossing it to the floor, as well. She placed his loose fist at the center of her chest, over her heart. His eyes widened at her gesture, but instead of pulling his hand away, he opened it, splaying his fingers over her breast.

"This is my heart," she said softly, holding his hand more tightly against her. With a shaky smile, she added, "You break it, mister, you've bought it."

Griffin opened his mouth to say something, but evidently decided against it. Instead he held up his other hand, silently encouraging Sarah to remove that glove, as well. She did so immediately, her fingers fumbling over the task this time because his hand curved over her breast completely, making languid circular motions that nearly drove her mad. The moment his other hand was free, Griffin swooped down on Sarah, pulling her into his arms and kissing her within an inch of her life.

She circled his neck with her arms to pull him closer, conveniently choosing to forget all the turmoil he'd caused her. His bare back was slick beneath her fingertips, and the perspiration on his chest soaked through her shirt to mingle with the dampness that had risen on her skin. She felt Griffin's hands under her shirt, skimming over the planes of her back, and she cried out with longing when they strummed over her rib cage and breasts. All at once, she remembered that they were standing in the gym at the police station and that anyone might wander in at any moment, including her friends and family. Immediately she pushed herself away from him, struggling to get herself under control.

"So," she said when she was able to manage speech again, "you, uh, you got any plans for the rest of the evening?"

His chest still rose and fell in an irregular rhythm, but he smiled. "Oh, yeah. You bet I have plans for the rest of the evening."

When he began to move toward her again, Sarah held up a hand and backed away. "Great. I'll see if Elaine can handle having the boys spend the night twice in one month." When he took another step forward, she took another step back. "And I'll wait for you while you shower and change," she added pointedly.

Griffin stooped to pick up the discarded boxing gloves and smashed cigar. "You know, this was a Cohiba," he said wistfully, indicating the crumpled heap of tobacco in his palm. "The last one in my great-grandfather's humidor."

"I'll get you another one," Sarah said apologetically. "A whole box of them."

He shook his head. "You can't get them here. They're Cuban."

She smiled. "Aren't Cuban cigars illegal in the U.S.?"

"Highly."

"Why, Detective," she cooed. "You are a lawless man, aren't you?"

He smiled back. "Well, my thoughts right now are anything but licit, that's certain."

He pushed past her and headed for the double doors through which she had come.

"Oh, Griffin," she called after him.

He turned, his expression inquisitive, but he said nothing.

Sarah chewed her lip nervously for some moments before voicing the question burning itself at the forefront of her brain. When he only stared at her silently, she drew in a deep, fortifying breath and asked, "Would you, uh...I mean, could you, er...that is..."

"Spit it out, Sarah."

"You won't by any chance have your...handcuffs...with you tonight, will you?"

The look on his face was positively profligate, and Sarah felt her temperature rise.

"Oh, Ms. Greenleaf," he said in the no-nonsense voice of efficiency she remembered from their very first encounter. "Just what kind of thoughts have you been entertaining?"

She lifted a shoulder in a noncommittal shrug, but said nothing. Griffin laughed, a deep, sensuous sound that reminded her of dark chocolate, then turned once again. She thought he would leave without replying, then he quickly spun around, returned and pulled her into his arms. With a single, roughly offered kiss, he released her and started off again.

She staggered backward and watched him go, wondering if she was as crazy as she felt, pursuing him this way. She'd never run after a man in her life, and discovered that there was a strange, heady delight that came with the chase. What she'd had with Michael had been a mutual admiration from the moment they'd met, and she hadn't met a man since her divorce who seemed worth the trouble. But Griffin was, she thought. He was something special, something wonderful, something she'd be crazy to let get away.

She was still tingling when she went to find Elaine and Stony. For the first time in her life, she thought, maybe, just maybe, something was going to work out the way it was supposed to.

Griffin felt good. Better than good—great. He stuffed the shirttail of his white T-shirt into faded Levi's and buttoned them up, hastily thrust his feet into well-worn boots and dragged a comb through his still damp hair. He was in a hurry. He had a date. A date with a woman who had tied him up in knots for weeks, a woman he couldn't get out of his head, a woman who would probably keep him feeling like a lovesick fool for the rest of his life.

As he collected the last of his things and zipped up his duffel bag, a flash of silver winked at him from the top shelf of his locker. He smiled as he reached up and lifted the handcuffs from their resting place. He wasn't sure if Sarah had been joking or not, but he sure as hell wasn't going to take any chances. Unzipping his duffel, he dropped the cuffs inside, then zipped it shut again and slung it over his shoulder. For some reason, he felt like belting out a few choruses of "Tonight, Tonight," but managed to contain himself. Taking a deep breath, he made his way out of the locker room and up to the squad room, where Sarah would be waiting for him.

As he took the steps two at a time, he thought about the night ahead. For the past sixteen days, he'd thought of little other than his one night with Sarah, had replayed in his head every touch and stroke over and over until he thought he would go mad with wanting her again. He'd planned what he'd do the next time they were alone together, had gone over it in his mind until he'd choreographed their lovemaking like a pro. All that was left was Sarah's input, and he had a feeling that her offering would be more than generous.

Tonight, he thought, would be even better than the last time. Tonight would be outstanding, unbelievable, amazing. Tonight...

He pushed through the double doors that led into the squad room and searched for Sarah, finding her immediately. She was watching him, smiling nervously, as if she, too, had been thinking about the night ahead. Oh, yes. They were definitely going to have an adventure.

"Griffin!"

A chorus of three small voices went up around him, and he suddenly realized Sarah wasn't alone. Jack and Sam sped out from behind Stony's desk, followed immediately by Jonah Bingham. The three boys rushed him, circling him like wild animals, inundating him with exclamations and questions.

"Jonah's spending the night with us tonight," Sam said.

"Mom said you might take us to the drive-in," Jack added. "They're showing *Bloodbath* and *Bloodbath, Part Two*."

Sarah quickly intervened. "I said we would *not* go see that, Jack. We'll let Griffin choose a movie." She looked up at him hopefully. "If he wants to."

Griffin stared at the four of them, confused, puzzled and utterly annoyed. "Uh, Sarah?" he asked softly.

She arched her brows inquisitively. "Yes?"

"Could I talk to you for a minute?"

"Certainly." She looked at him silently, expectantly, but did not move from her frozen position.

"Alone?" he clarified.

Her eyes widened, giving her an almost panicked look, but she nodded quickly. Still, however, she did not move. He lifted his left hand palm up, closing his fist except for his index finger, which he crooked in that ages-old, somewhat ominous gesture.

"Boys?" Sarah said to the still-squirming youngsters, her voice cracking a little on the word. "Can you sit quietly here at Mr. Stonestreet's desk while I have a little talk with Griffin?''

"Sure," Jack said with a shrug before leading the others back to the bulletin board. He pointed to one photo, urging Jonah to look more closely. "It's Mr. Pike, I tell ya. Look at the guy's nose."

Griffin took advantage of their rapt attention elsewhere to grab Sarah's wrist and pull her along behind him. When they were safely out of earshot, he turned, settled his hands on his hips and demanded, "What the hell is going on here?"

"I'm really sorry," she began. "But when I got back up here, Elaine and Stony were having a kind of, um, *intense* conversation, and Elaine asked me if I could keep Jonah for the night."

"And you said yes?" Griffin asked incredulously. "After we...I mean, after the plans we made?"

Now Sarah placed her hands on her own hips, mirroring his challenging posture. "Well, I couldn't very well say no, could I?" she replied. "She kept Jack and Sam last time so that you and I could..." Two bright spots of pink colored her cheeks when she halted. "So that you and I could be alone," she finished hastily. "Tonight she and Stony needed some time alone, and it's my turn to take sleep-over duty. But if you dislike my children so much—"

"Oh, no, you don't," he said. "I like your kids just fine and you know it. It's just..."

"What?"

Griffin drew in a deep, impatient breath, and raked his fingers through his hair. "I wanted *us* to be alone. I wanted to..." He cupped his hands over her shoulders and started to pull her close, looked past her to see her two sons and their best friend watching them intently and dropped his hands back to his sides again. "Dammit, I wanted to make love to you tonight."

Sarah bit her lip, and he could tell she was trying not to laugh. "You hopeless romantic, you. You really know how to sweet-talk a girl."

"No, Sarah, I meant—"

But she held up a hand to stop him. "I wanted that, too," she said with a smile. "But you're about to learn that when you have kids, you can't always have what you want. In fact," she added, glancing over her shoulder, "you hardly ever get what you want."

"Then why don't you send them off to boarding school?" he asked, only half-joking.

She laughed. "Well, the subject of the military academy did come up frequently between Michael and me, but..." She shrugged. "So what do you say, Griffin? You want to go to the drive-in with me?"

"With you and three other guys?"

She nodded.

"I suppose necking in the back seat would be out of the question."

"Completely."

He sighed again. "Oh, all right. But you have to buy the popcorn."

She threaded her fingers through his and pulled him along behind her as she went to rejoin the boys. As she herded the three youngsters out ahead of them, she turned back to tell Griffin, "Did I mention that they usually fall asleep during the first half?"

He felt a flicker of optimism ignite somewhere in the dark recesses of his heart. Maybe, just maybe, there was hope for the night yet.

Eight

Sarah listened to the chaotic thumping and squealing of three excited—and wide-awake—boys in her sons' bedroom upstairs, stared at Griffin stretched out fast asleep on her living room sofa and sighed. She supposed she should wake him and send him home; it was past one o'clock. But he looked so peaceful lying there—as if this was the first decent night's sleep he'd had in ages. She couldn't quite bring herself to rouse him. So she sat in the big club chair opposite him and watched him sleep, trying to ignore how utterly right it felt to do something so simple and harmless.

She couldn't recall a single moment during her marriage when she had felt as peaceful as she did at that moment. Virtually from day one after marrying Michael, she had experienced some anxiety, some feeling that she'd made a mistake, however small the fear may have been. But from the second she had seen Griffin Lawless standing in her kitchen doorway the night of the Cub Scout meeting, the second she had realized he had every intention of kissing her, she had known—somehow she had just *known*—that whatever was going to happen between them would be the right thing.

He stirred a little, uttering a soft, sleepy sound as he shifted on the sofa, then brought one muscular forearm up to rest it over his eyes. Yet he did not awaken.

"Griffin?" she asked quietly. She didn't want to disturb him, but knew she really should make some effort to wake him. When he did not reply, she tried once more.

"Oh, Griffin?" she asked again, drawing his name out on a long, low whisper.

He grunted, but offered no further indication that he'd heard her.

Sarah stood and went to a closet in the hall, pulled down a lightweight blanket and returned to the living room. He had removed his boots while she was upstairs getting the boys settled down, and now the dusty, creased leather accessories sat on the floor beside the couch. So she draped the blanket carefully over him from chest to toe, switched off the lamp at his head and tiptoed quietly out of the room.

"Good night, Griffin," she said over her shoulder as she left.

"'Night, sweetheart," he mumbled after her in his sleep.

Griffin awoke to a very strange noise—that of children laughing. Or more specifically, he realized as he opened one eye, children laughing at *him*. Standing over him were Sarah's two sons and their friend, who he had last seen in Sarah's living room the night before when she had ordered them all upstairs to bed. So what were they doing in his apartment now?

Griffin opened his other eye and fixed his gaze on a huge ceiling fan swirling laconically above him. He didn't have a ceiling fan, he recalled vaguely. Staring down at the lightweight blanket clutched in his hands, he remembered that he didn't have any bed linens that were pink, either.

"Mom!" Jack shouted only inches away from Griffin's ear. "He's awake! Now can we ask him?"

He heard Sarah's reply from the kitchen, but couldn't quite understand the words. He looked to Jack for clarification.

"You want syrup or jam with your waffles?"

"Waffles?" Griffin asked, still a little fuzzy. He'd never been one for quick coherence in the morning.

The boy nodded. "Mom's fixing waffles, but she's running late for work, so you gotta pick fast. Syrup or jam?"

"Syrup," Griffin answered automatically. Immediately the three boys ran off, and he was left to wonder yet again what the hell was going on.

He jackknifed up into a sitting position, scrubbed his hands quickly over his face and shook his head to clear it. Slowly memories of the previous evening began to form an orderly picture in his mind. He had fallen asleep on Sarah's couch, he realized, something that wasn't supposed to have happened. He had intended to wait for her while she got the boys tucked in and then he had planned to neck with her on this very couch for a long, long time after the three little imps had fallen asleep. Apparently, however, the three little imps had outlasted him.

He stumbled to the kitchen and saw Sarah standing at the counter beside the toaster, eyeing it expectantly and waiting for something. She was wearing a bright red, dress-for-success suit, sheer hose and no shoes. In one hand she held a dinner plate, in the other a blunt knife covered with what looked to be strawberry jam. Griffin was about to say good-morning, when the toaster clicked, two amber squares shot up from its slots and she caught them deftly on the plate before slathering them with jam. This was clearly a routine she had choreographed with great results some time ago, and he marveled at her graceful moves as she set the plate down in front of Sam.

"Thanks, Mom," the little boy said before digging into his breakfast.

"Good morning," Griffin said as he watched her shake two more frozen waffles from a box and tuck them into the toaster.

She turned to greet him with a quick, shy smile. "Good morning. Would you like some coffee?"

"Please."

The mug she pressed against his palm was warm, the coffee inside smelling strong and rich. The fragrance alone did wonders in bringing him back to life. He placed his fingers over hers as she transferred the mug to his possession, reveling in the touch, however brief.

"Sorry I fell asleep on you last night," he said. "I guess I was more tired than I realized."

She shrugged it off. "That's okay. I was going to wake you, but you were sleeping so soundly, I didn't have the heart to disturb you."

He nodded, sipped his coffee and tried to think of something to say. He'd never awakened in a woman's home to find that woman's children looking on. He would have thought such a situation would feel awkward and uncomfortable. He would have thought he'd be annoyed to find himself surrounded by a bunch of little kids when all he really wanted to do was wrestle Sarah to the floor and have his way with her.

Instead he was overcome by a giddy sense of well-being unlike anything he'd ever felt before. Of course, he still wanted to have his way with Sarah, but knowing he'd have to wait, knowing he'd be forced to tolerate the anticipation, somehow made the wanting even more intense—more pleasurable—than usual.

When he still could think of nothing mind-boggling or earth-shattering to say, he simply voiced the first thought that popped into his head. "You look incredible."

Sarah glanced up and ran a quick hand through her tousled curls. "Thanks," she said softly. "I have a meeting with a client this morning."

"I'll say you do."

She blushed, then chuckled a little nervously. "No, not you." He hoped he wasn't imagining that regretful tone in her voice. "I mean a different client."

"Oh." He also hoped his own disappointment wasn't too obvious.

She was about to say something more, but the toaster clicked again, and she rushed back to retrieve her breakfast. For a moment, Griffin thought she was going to miss the waffles fast descending from their graceful arc through the air, but she managed at just the last minute to get the plate into position.

"I suppose I really should take the toaster in for repairs," she said. "Surely this isn't the way it's supposed to work."

"Nah," Griffin countered. "That would take all the fun out of breakfast."

"True. Have a seat," she instructed him as she set the plate before one of the two remaining empty places at the table. "Sorry they're frozen, but the last time I tried to make waffles from scratch, uh..." Her voice trailed off as she went to refill her coffee cup.

Jack completed the sentence for her. "The firemen made her promise she'd never do it again," he said before stuffing another bite of waffle into his mouth.

"It really wasn't my fault," Sarah said. "It was the waffle iron. A frayed cord. Honest. The explosion had nothing to do with the recipe. It was my mother's recipe, for pete's—"

"Explosion?" Griffin interrupted.

She nodded, but didn't elaborate further.

He shook his head. "Well, as long as no one was injured."

"No, not really."

"Mom just got her eyebrows singed a little is all," Sam said. "They grew back okay, though."

Griffin couldn't help but laugh as he reached for the syrup. "In that case, I urge you not to go to any trouble for me. I usually skip breakfast entirely."

"Eat fast, you guys," Sarah said to the boys. "Mrs. MacAfee will be here any minute, and I want to have the dishes done before she arrives." She glanced at her watch, her expression anxious. "And if she doesn't get here soon, I'm going to be late."

"Why don't you go ahead?" Griffin told her. "I can keep an eye on the boys until your sitter gets here. And I promise to wash the dishes."

"Oh, thanks, but I couldn't ask you to—"

"It's no trouble. I don't have to be at work for another hour."

"But you have to go home first, and—"

"Sarah," he interrupted her again. "I wouldn't offer if it was going to be an imposition."

She smiled gratefully. "Thanks. I owe you one."

He smiled back. "I'll be sure to collect. Soon."

She hurried from the kitchen, but not before throwing him a lascivious look. Griffin smiled at how easily he seemed to have become a part of her morning routine. He studied the boys surrounding him at the table, then looked down at the food on his plate. This morning was unlike any other he'd ever spent, and he liked the feeling of starting the day off in such a way—with other people. Especially other people like Sarah and her kids.

"So what do you guys have planned for today?" he asked the boys.

Jack replied enthusiastically, "They're building a new subdivision over off Heath Lane, so we're gonna ride our bikes over and watch."

"Then what are you going to do?"

Jack shrugged. "After they leave for the day, we can play on the dirt piles."

Griffin nodded. He vaguely recalled a time in his life when he could spend an entire day in one place, finding a million things to do. "Sounds like fun," he said, wishing for some reason that he could take the day off and join them at the construction site, watching the bulldozers shift the earth and hurling dirt clods in a fight to defend the neighborhood.

Sarah came in amid a clacking of heels on the tile floor, affixing a gold earring in her ear. She treated each of her sons to a kiss on the forehead, wiped a slathering of jam from Sam's face, then, with a hastily offered farewell, headed for the back door.

"Hey," Griffin called after her, rising to follow.

As she pivoted quickly to face him, he wondered if what he intended to do was wise. Wise or not, however, he couldn't keep himself from framing her face in his hands and leaning forward to kiss her briefly on the lips. He knew the boys were watching with great interest, knew she would probably belt him for making the intimate gesture in their presence. But kissing Sarah goodbye as she left for work seemed like the most natural thing in the world for him to do.

"Have a good day," he said softly. "And be careful."

She covered his hands lightly with her own, but did not push them away. In her eyes, he detected any number of confused, conflicting emotions, emotions he figured pretty well mirrored his own. He smiled, hoping his expression was more reassuring than he felt.

"Thanks," she replied quietly. "I will."

They both dropped their hands back to their sides, then stood staring at each other awkwardly. Their relationship had just taken a giant step forward with that one brief kiss, and now neither of them seemed to be sure where to go next.

Sarah was the first to glance away, turning her attention to the boys. "You all be good for Griffin, okay? And don't give Mrs. MacAfee a hard time, either."

Three pairs of very wide, very curious eyes gazed back at them, and all three boys nodded enthusiastically. Griffin could tell she was trying to hide her smile when she turned back toward him.

"'Bye," she said.

"'Bye."

And then she was gone, and all that remained was a faint scent of flowers and a warm feeling that spiraled up from somewhere deep in Griffin's heart. He felt the penetrating gaze of the three boys as he went back to his seat, but he said nothing, instead opting to see what their reaction would be. Jonah quickly went back to eating, while Sam and Jack exchanged interested looks. Jack would be the first to speak up, Griffin thought. It was simply the boy's nature to be the bold one. He held his breath and waited.

He didn't have to wait long.

Jack studied him intently as he asked, "Do you like my mom?"

Griffin nodded. "Yes. Yes, I do."

"You gonna marry her?"

Griffin's fork halted halfway to his mouth, syrup dripping from the waffle. Well, that was a question he hadn't expected to hear. Obviously he had underestimated the power of a child's curiosity. "Uh," he began.

"Well?" Jack asked.

Griffin recalled those awkward moments as a teenager, when he had been forced to undergo the third degree of a worried father before being allowed to date the man's daughter. He had never been comfortable stating his intentions toward a girl. And now as he levelly met the gaze of the freckle-faced eight-year-old seated opposite him, his palms began to sweat.

"'Cause Mom likes you, too," Jack went on. "I can tell. I think you should marry her."

"She's not a very good cook," Sam added parenthetically, "but she's kinda pretty."

"And she likes baseball," Jack said.

"And basketball."

"And hockey, too."

"She's real funny."

"And she buys Snickers candy bars to give out on Halloween."

"And," Sam concluded, as if this were the most important quality of all, "she might let you have a puppy if you can keep your room clean for a whole year."

Griffin stared at the two boys, wondering how in the hell he'd gotten himself into this one. "Well, boys," he began, stalling for time. "Your mom's great and all. I like her a lot. But I'm not sure if—"

The telephone rang then, delivering him like a miracle descended from the heavens. Griffin leaped up to grab it, barking out a grateful hello, then frowned when no one replied from the other end of the line.

"Hello?" he asked again.

"Hello?" the voice replied. Whoever she was, Griffin thought, she sounded like she was at death's door. "I'm trying to reach Sarah Greenleaf."

"This is the Greenleaf residence," he said. "Sarah's gone to work. I'm staying with her sons until the sitter gets here."

"Well, I'm Dana MacAfee, the sitter," the woman said. "And I'm calling to tell Sarah I won't be able to make it in today."

"Oh?"

"No, I'm sorry. I've come down with something perfectly horrible and no doubt highly contagious. I don't think it would be a good idea for me to sit with the boys."

"I see."

"I hope this won't create any problems."

"No, none at all," Griffin said, wondering what to do.

"Please give Sarah my apologies."

"I will. And I hope you feel better," he added as an afterthought, before hooking the phone receiver back into its cradle.

Now what? he wondered. He had no idea where Sarah was going to be, and he couldn't very well leave three eight-year-old boys to their own devices all day. Could he? No, of course not. Even if they'd be doing nothing more than running around the neighborhood on their own, there had to be someone here for them to contact if they got hurt or into trouble. That gave Griffin pause. What if one of them did get hurt? The very idea made him cringe.

"Who was that?" Jack asked.

"Mrs. MacAfee," Griffin told him. "She's sick. She won't be able to come over today."

"Yaaaaaaay!" The cheers went up all around him, and he had to hide his smile.

"You shouldn't cheer when someone's sick," he told the boys. "It's not very nice."

They sobered somewhat, but not much.

He sighed, recognizing only one solution to the problem. "So I guess that means you're stuck with me for the day. What would you three like to do?"

Why he had just appointed himself baby-sitter, Griffin had no idea. Certainly Stony and his sergeant wouldn't be too thrilled about his missing a day of work to keep an eye on three kids. Still, the Jerwal case was just about tied up. Stony could gather the loose ends on his own, and by tomorrow, they'd probably be ready to make the arrests. The realization that he would be arresting the uncle of two of the boys he'd be watching today—not to mention the brother of the woman in whose life he was feeling so unbelievably comfortable lately—did not sit well with Griffin, so he pushed the thought away. Instead he focused his attention on the youngsters who stared back at him.

"Well?" he asked. "What'll it be?"

He watched as all three boys exchanged glances, then was amazed as three identical smiles broke out in unison. Griffin smiled back, but for some reason felt a little wary. There was something about those smiles...

"Firestorm!" the boys shouted as one.

"Firestorm?" Griffin asked. "What's that?"

Jack lifted a shoulder in a nonchalant shrug. "Oh, it's just a movie is all," he said.

Griffin was relieved. He'd been afraid it was some dangerous new ride at the amusement park. "Oh. Okay," he said. "We'll go see *Firestorm*."

"Yes!" the boys chorused with high-fives all around.

This was going to be a piece of cake, Griffin thought. If all they wanted to do was go to the movies, they'd go to the movies. This kid stuff was kid stuff. Nothing to it. He thought about what would happen later, when Sarah came home to find that he had spent the day with her children and had taken them to a movie they'd wanted to see. He thought about how pleased she'd be by the new camaraderie. He smiled.

"Just let me make a couple of phone calls," he said to the boys. "Then we can be on our way."

The last thing Sarah expected to see when she arrived home from work was Griffin Lawless standing barefoot in her kitchen, wearing a frilly apron covered with a cat print over his khaki shorts and navy blue T-shirt and stirring something that smelled wonderfully like barbecue. Nevertheless, that was exactly the sight that greeted her when she came through her back door Tuesday evening.

"Hi," she said as she latched the screen door behind her.

Griffin turned quickly at the sound of her voice, looking extremely guilty about something. His movements were jerky as he tapped the spoon against the pot and laid it on the spoon rest, and he made no move to approach her. Instead he leaned back against the counter, gripping it fiercely as if it were trying to escape. And although he smiled, his expression was in no way happy or reassuring.

"What's wrong?" she asked. "What are you doing here? Where's Mrs. MacAfee? Where are the boys?"

Evidently he chose to answer her questions in the reverse order they were asked, because he began, "The boys said they were going to ride over to the new subdivision, but I told them to be home by six. Mrs. MacAfee called in sick.

Since I didn't know where to reach you, I took the day off to watch the boys."

"Oh, Griffin, I am so sorry about that," Sarah apologized. "You could have called Elaine at the shop. She could have told you where I was. Or better yet, she could have come for the boys herself."

"Elaine had to work, too," he said.

"And so did you," she reminded him.

He shrugged off her concern. "It was no trouble to take the day off. Stony understood."

She doubted it had been as easy as he made it sound. "I owe you another big one."

For the first time, his smile was genuine. "This is becoming a pretty big debt you owe me. We'll have to start discussing the terms of repayment soon."

Sarah felt herself grow warm at the way he was looking at her and, in an effort to steer the conversation back into safe waters, said, "So if everything worked out all right, how come you look like you spent the day on a chain gang?"

Griffin's smile fell again, and he turned his attention back to whatever it was he was cooking. "I, uh," he began. He glanced up quickly, but apparently was uncomfortable meeting her gaze, because, just as quickly, he glanced down at the pot again. He inhaled a deep breath, released it slowly, then tried once more. "I think I may have done a bad thing today."

Sarah doubted he was capable of doing anything bad, in spite of his bad-boy appearance, which had at one time so intimidated her. "Well," she began as she kicked off her shoes and shrugged out of her jacket, unbuttoning the top two buttons of her blouse. "Considering the fact that you spent the day with my kids, that's not entirely surprising. What was it this time? Grand-theft auto? Civil rebellion? World War III?"

"Ah, actually," Griffin said, "it was a movie."

Knowing her sons as well as she did, she immediately understood. "Don't tell me, let me guess You asked them what they wanted to do, and they told you to take them to see that new adventure flick.''

"*Firestorm,*" he stated apologetically.

"That's the one.''

"Sarah, I promise you I had no idea what kind of movie it was. I thought it had those turtle things in it or something. If I'd known about the other stuff—''

"The women with big hooters?'' she supplied helpfully.

He halted, mouth gaping, as if this newly offered bit of information was too troubling to consider. "There were women with big hooters in that movie?''

"Don't tell me you didn't notice.''

He shook his head. "I gathered up the boys less than a half hour into the movie and hurried them out because the violence was unbelievable. And the language...'' He shook his head helplessly, as if still haunted by the memory. "I mean, I don't hear stuff that bad in the locker room at the station. Good God, if I'd had to explain to the boys about hooters, too...'' He shuddered visibly. "What are people thinking to make movies like that?''

Sarah's heart turned over at his undeniable shock and horror at what the situation with her children might have become. She stood on tiptoe and kissed his cheek. "You're a good guy, Griffin,'' she said before pulling back.

But he didn't let her go far. Before she could get away, he cupped his hand around her neck and pulled her back toward him. She was assailed by the spicy, masculine fragrance that was so essentially Griffin, felt the heat of his body mingling with hers. Her pulse rate quickened as she drew nearer, and she closed her eyes lest she be overcome by the desire winding its way up from somewhere deep inside her. It was amazing, she thought vaguely, how quickly things could go from harmless to dangerous where such a lawless man was concerned.

"So you're not angry with me for jeopardizing the moral well-being of your children?'' he asked her softly, his mouth scant inches away from her ear.

She smiled, opening her eyes again simply to enjoy the sight of him. "With you?" she replied, hoping she didn't sound as breathless as she felt. "No, I'm not angry with you. You couldn't have known what you were getting yourself into. Jack and Sam, on the other hand, knew exactly what they were doing. I told them quite specifically that that movie was off-limits, and they suckered you into taking them, anyway."

Now Griffin smiled. "Don't be too rough on them. I would have done the same thing when I was a kid."

Sarah knew she would have, too, but that was beside the point. Her sons were in for a good talking to. "So is this why you're in here cooking dinner? Because you feel guilty about exposing my sons to the seamier side of life?"

With his free hand, Griffin tangled his fingers with hers, then lifted her hand to his lips. "Well, that and the fact that I wanted to impress you." He touched his tongue to the juncture between her thumb and index finger.

Sarah closed her eyes as a shudder of delight worked its way through her body. "Impress me?" she managed to whisper.

"Mm-hmm."

He skimmed his lips over her palm, kissed her wrist, then journeyed up her arm to the inside of her elbow. As he moved higher, Sarah pulled her sleeve back to grant him more complete access, then curved her hand over his nape to pull him closer. She sighed when he straightened and kissed the side of her neck.

"Oh, I'm very impressed," she said softly.

"Really?"

She nodded, the scrape of his day-old beard against her sensitive skin raising goose bumps. "Mmm" was all she was able to manage in response.

"You know," he began, his voice a quiet vibration against her neck, "Jack mentioned something today about how he and Sam spend a month with their father every summer. I, uh, I don't suppose that month is coming up anytime soon is it?"

Sarah shook her head slowly, trying to get a better focus of her muddled, feverish thoughts. "What day is this?" she asked.

"I'm not sure," he said. "The twenty-eighth? Twenty-ninth?"

"They won't be going to stay with their father until the first of August, so that's what . . . ?" For some reason, with Griffin nibbling on her earlobe that way, she was having trouble figuring her math.

He groaned. "Four weeks away."

Sarah glanced down at her watch. "You, uh, you told the boys to be home at six?" It was only five-twenty. That gave them a whole forty minutes to—

"Yes," Griffin interrupted her racing thoughts.

She tugged at the apron strings knotted behind his waist. "You know, a lot can happen in forty minutes."

He nodded, lifting his hands to work at the pearly buttons on her blouse. "Yes, it can."

The apron fell to the floor just as he freed the last button from its loop. He pulled her fiercely against him, kissing her with a hunger and need that rivaled her own. Sarah tangled her fingers in the dark silk of his hair, pulling him closer, until she felt the fullness of him pressing against her belly. When she realized how ready he was for her, she moaned, dropping her hands to his taut buttocks to pull him closer still. He curved his hand over her breast, thumbing the sensitive peak to life. She was just about to suggest they turn off the stove and duck back into her bedroom, when she heard the squeak of a bicycle kickstand out in the driveway beyond the back door, followed by Jack's high-pitched yell.

"Mom! Sam fell off his bike again and skinned his knee!"

The couple sprang apart as if someone had just doused them both with a fire hose. Griffin scooped up the apron from the floor and quickly tied it around himself again, and

Sarah hoped the thin scrap of fabric would be enough to camouflage his condition. She fumbled with the buttons on her blouse until they were—she hoped—suitably refastened, then pushed a handful of blond curls back from her face. Unable to meet Griffin's gaze, she worried instead about striking what she hoped would be a nonchalant pose before her sons came bursting through the back door.

She gave Sam's knee a brief inspection, pronounced the wound not life threatening, then, with a quick kiss on his cheek, sent the boys off to the bathroom for the disinfectant spray and a Band-Aid. Sam was sniffling a little, more scared than hurt, she thought, and Jack draped a reassuring arm over his brother's shoulder as they made their way down the hall.

"They're good kids," Sarah said as she turned to Griffin. "But they have very bad timing."

He smiled at her, then looked at the pot on the stove and sighed deeply. "It's just as well. The barbecue is starting to burn."

Sarah bit her lip to keep from commenting that the barbecue wasn't the only thing in the house burning. Instead she said, "I'll just go check on Sam. Make sure Jack hasn't bandaged him within an inch of his life."

She waited for Griffin to reply, but he only nodded. She made it as far as the doorway before he called out her name. She halted, glancing back over her shoulder.

"I won't wait until August 1," he said without turning around.

She drew a shaky breath. "You won't have to," she told him. And before either of them had a chance to comment further, she bolted from the room.

Nine

The following Thursday found Sarah picking through the last of the items she'd discovered in the china cabinet of Judge Mercer's formal dining room—formal, as opposed to the smaller, more intimate family dining room in another wing of the house. Since she'd never done an appraisal for anyone before, she had tried to be organized for once in her life while performing the task for Griffin. She had started in the west wing of the house, working from the attic down. Now, more than four weeks after beginning her task, she had just begun to explore the first floor of the house. One thing was certain. No matter what happened between Griffin and her in their personal lives, she would be tied to him professionally for a good while yet.

Because she was no longer digging around in crates and straw-filled boxes, she now tried to dress as professionally as possible for work, and had opted today for a white blouse and no-nonsense, tailored blue skirt. Nonetheless, she hadn't been able to keep herself from kicking off her shoes and now sat barefoot before the china cabinet. She was dismayed that she had still managed to pick up a few smudges of dust and grime, and was rubbing at a spot of black on her hem, when she looked inside the cabinet and saw something wonderful. The light from the chandelier above her glinted off a crystal vase as if it had been manufactured from stardust. Sarah held her breath as she reached inside.

She pulled the piece slowly from its resting place and gave it a thorough inspection before confirming the conclusion she had already leaped to. What she held was a Lalique vase, approximately twenty-four inches in height, crystal clear at the top, etched with a frosty rendition of Artemis and animals where the belly flared out. It was signed and numbered by the artist and looked brand-new. But the artist in question had created pieces for the company more than a century ago, and although his work had been coveted in the collecting community, very little of it remained. Should the piece be authentic—and she was certain it was—the vase was worth several hundred thousand dollars.

She whistled low under her breath, turning the piece carefully in her hands, lifting it in the direction of a window to let the clear segment of the crystal catch the light. She gasped as a single ray of sunshine exploded into a brilliant cascade of rainbow hues that danced on the wall above her. The vase should be in a museum, she thought, suddenly realizing the enormity of what she held in her hands. She wondered how long it had been in the Mercer family, wondered how much had originally been spent to acquire it.

"Wow."

The word thundered through the cavernous, empty room from somewhere behind her, and so rapt had been her attention on the vase that Sarah started at the sound of Griffin's voice. For the briefest of moments, the vase began to slip from her fingers, and she quickly wrapped her free arm around it and pulled it to her breast. She rose up on her knees and twisted around to look at him. He was leaning in the doorway on the opposite side of the room, wearing his detective uniform of rumpled gray trousers, rumpled white shirt and wrinkled necktie. She wondered if he owned an iron.

"Oh, God, Griffin," she groaned. "Don't ever sneak up on me like that again."

He smiled as he pushed himself away from the doorjamb and started toward her. "Why not? I like to watch you jump."

"Yeah, well, my jump this time could have cost you more than half a million dollars."

He stopped in midstride, his gaze wandering from her face to the crystal vase she still clutched in her arms like a newborn baby. *"What?"*

She nodded, extending the piece out as far as she dared for his inspection. "This little trinket right here could net you a very tidy sum. I mean, collectively speaking, the contents of this house have already made you a millionaire several times over, but if Judge Mercer has anything else like this stowed away, you could be looking at some *really* serious dough."

Griffin stared at Sarah for a long time, letting her words sink in. Until that moment, he honestly hadn't allowed himself to consider the magnitude of all that his until-recently-unknown relative had left to him. But as he heard her voice it in such matter-of-fact terms and saw the undeniably exquisite richness of the vase she held in her hands, the knowledge of what had befallen him hit him like a ton of bricks, and he felt his knees begin to crumple beneath him.

Before he embarrassed himself by toppling over, Griffin dropped to sit on the floor beside Sarah, extending a finger to trace it carefully over the fine crystal vase.

"Half a million?" he echoed.

She nodded. "At least."

"That's unbelievable."

"Believe it."

He shook his head in wonder, trying his best to cope with the montage of emotions swirling around in his head. He had come to the house to find Sarah because he and Stony had finally received the warrants for the arrests of Wallace Greenleaf and Jerry Schmidt. He had wanted to tell her what was going to happen before he and Stony swooped in to cart her brother off to jail. He knew a confrontation with Sarah would doubtlessly ensue. He knew she'd be angry with him and might not want to see him for a long time. And hell, he wouldn't exactly blame her.

But he had wanted to prepare her, and had wanted a chance to state his case before she drew the wrong conclusions. And, he admitted sheepishly, he'd wanted to let her know just what a crook her brother was before Wally had a chance to defend himself.

Okay, so maybe that wasn't very nice of him, being a part of the justice system as he was. But some things were more important than technical legalities, right? Love, for example, was supposed to conquer all, was it not?

But somehow, the words that Griffin needed to speak escaped him. As he looked at Sarah, sitting in this magnificent house—a house that was his but didn't feel as if it was—holding a work of art worth so much money, a work of art that was also his but didn't feel as if it was, Griffin wanted to claim Sarah as his own, too. Unequivocally, irretrievably. He didn't feel as if he belonged amid the glorious Mercer holdings. But he did feel as if he belonged with Sarah. He only hoped she'd still want him after she realized what he'd done.

Without thinking about his feelings, he reached out and cradled the vase in his hands, then placed it carefully back inside the open china cabinet. Moving quickly, so that he didn't have time to think about his actions, he rose and extended his hand to Sarah. She looked at him questioningly before touching her fingers to his, but his silence must have encouraged her to remain quiet, too.

He helped her to her feet and immediately pulled her into his arms, ducking his head to kiss her. But what he'd intended to be a simple gesture, a soft caress, was nothing less than a heart-stopping joining of his mouth with hers. He kissed her hard, fast, deep and long, because for some reason he suddenly couldn't get enough of her. His fingers entwined around her nape, then tangled in her blond curls, pushing her head even closer to his so that he could plunder the dark recesses of her mouth more fully. But still it wasn't enough.

Finally Sarah tore her mouth from his, gasping for breath. "Griffin, please. I can hardly breathe."

But instead of accommodating her request, he kissed her again, with all the ferocity of the first time. He wound an arm around her waist, working feverishly at the buttons on her blouse with his free hand. She helped him yank her shirttail free of her skirt, then guided his hand to the front clasp of her lacy brassiere. Her skin was warm and soft, and he felt her heartbeat raging out of control beneath his fingertips. He moved his hand to the right until he cupped her breast in his hand, then traced his thumb in slow, insistent circles over the taut peak.

She moaned at the intimate touch, arching against him to give him freer access. An explosion of white light burst somewhere in Griffin's brain, and afterward all coherent thought fled him. All he wanted was to be with Sarah. Nothing, nothing else in the world, mattered otherwise.

"I love you, Sarah," he whispered against her mouth.

He wasn't sure he wanted to hear her response, so he kissed her again, as deeply as before. He felt her tugging frantically at his belt, and pulled away from her enough to facilitate her efforts. With deft fingers, she found her way inside, cupping what she could of him in her palm before stroking her fingers up and down against him.

This time Griffin was the one to groan, pausing in his exploration of Sarah to enjoy the exquisite sensations her hand wreaked upon him. He didn't understand the sudden intensity of his desire for her, couldn't fathom why she above all others should be the woman he couldn't live without. He only knew he needed her, right here, right now, for as long as it took to satisfy their hunger, for as long as it took to make them both happy forever.

"Upstairs," he managed to whisper as he panted for breath. "There are bedrooms upstairs."

Sarah, too, was panting, but tilted her head back to look at him. "Did you come as prepared this afternoon as you were at my house that night?"

He smiled and nodded.

She smiled back. "Did you bring your handcuffs?"

He chuckled. "They're out in the car."

"Pity." She sighed wistfully. "Well, next time for sure."

Griffin scooped her up in his arms and headed for the stairs, taking them two at a time and stopping at the first door he encountered. The bedroom smelled dusty and old, but the bright afternoon sun beat down through the window, throwing an irregular rectangle of light across the flowered coverlet on the bed. He wondered briefly who the room had belonged to so many years ago, wondered if perhaps it was Meredith's room, the room where his mother had been born.

But his thoughts quickly turned toward a new avenue when he looked down at Sarah, at the blond curls mussed by his touch, the lips reddened by his kisses. Their disarrayed clothing reminded him of how close he was to completely losing control. He released her slowly, rubbing his body languorously against hers as he set her down, then swooped in to kiss her again.

Sarah was blindsided by that kiss. One minute she was leaning heavily against Griffin, gripping his big biceps to prevent her knees from buckling beneath her, and the next she was lost in a wondrous embrace. He cupped his hands over her shoulders, pressed his flattened palms intimately down her back, then curved his fingers over her derriere and pushed her insistently against him. She felt the swollen length of him pressing against her abdomen, and recalled in an unusually vivid memory what it had been like to feel him inside her the first time. Her temperature soared at the reminder, heat writhing through her before pooling at the juncture of her thighs. She tangled her fingers in his hair to pull him closer, returning his kiss as deeply as he had offered it, trying to devour him before he could consume her.

She struggled with his necktie until she had yanked it free of his shirt, then fumbled to undo his buttons. After a moment she felt his fingers join hers in the task, then she splayed her hands wide over the warm, rigid expanse of his chest as Griffin shrugged out of his shirt. He was a magnificent creature, she thought vaguely, marveling again at the way the muscles bunched and moved beneath her fingertips as if they were alive. Her fingers tripped down over his rib cage, pausing at the waistband of his trousers before venturing onward. Griffin caught her hands in his before she could explore further, however, and he chuckled low.

"Not yet," he said softly. "I'm liable to go off like a bazooka, and I don't want that to happen until I'm finished with you."

Her heart thumped wildly at the promise of more intimacies to come, but she smiled. "Oh?" she asked. "And just what did you have in mind for me?"

He smiled back, a smile that was at once salacious, seductive and serene. "Just you wait and see."

Without a moment's hesitation, he pushed her blouse and brassiere from her shoulders, ignoring the garments as they floated to the floor in a white heap beside his shirt. Carefully, as if he were reaching for the crystal vase he had so recently cradled in his hands, he covered her breasts with warm fingers. At first he only held her that way, his eyes never leaving hers, then he thumbed the tumid peaks to greater life. She was helpless to prevent the single sound of delight she emitted, and Griffin smiled. He bent forward and pressed his lips against the flesh he touched, drawing

one velvety breast to his mouth, circling her with his tongue
before tugging her more deeply inside.

For long moments he suckled her, driving her closer and
closer to the brink. Just when she thought she could no
longer tolerate the sensations shuddering through her, he
pulled away, pausing to place one quick kiss over her heart
before turning his attentions elsewhere.

He reached around behind her and tugged down the zipper on her skirt, kneeling before her as he shoved it down
around her ankles. Before she could step out of it, he
gripped her waist in his hands, holding her in place. He
leaned forward, pressing his mouth to the soft cotton fabric of her panties, exhaling a hot, damp breath before kissing her through the thin fabric. Then he hooked his thumbs
in the waistband and pulled them down, too. But instead of
rising, he lifted one of her feet from their confinement,
urged her legs apart and settled his hands on her waist again.

It had been hot in the bedroom when they'd entered,
Sarah thought absently as she cupped her hands over Griffin's shoulders to steady herself. But not nearly as hot as it
became when she looked down to watch Griffin's dark head
descend upon her again. With every piercing stroke of his
tongue against that most intimate part of her, the bedroom
grew warmer, until she was certain it had become engulfed
in flame. She squeezed Griffin's shoulders more tightly and
tilted her head back to gaze at the ceiling. The bedroom was
fine, she noted as her eyes fluttered closed. It was only she
who had succumbed to the fire.

Just as she reached the white-hot center of that heat, she
cried out loud, and Griffin finally ended his onslaught. He
kissed her flat belly, dipped his tongue into her navel, then
raked his hands up over her rib cage to cover her breasts.
Slowly he rose, towering over her, and she wondered how on
earth she had ever gotten by without this man in her life. She
started to speak, but he lifted two fingers to her lips, halt-
ing any words she might have uttered. He reached for her
hand, twining their fingers, then rubbed her open palm over

the rigid swell in his trousers. He gasped, tilting his head back, and Sarah took a step closer.

When he released her hand, she continued the primal rhythm he had started, until she could no longer tolerate the distance between them. Together they removed what remained of his clothing, and together they moved toward the bed. They had scarcely pushed the covers to the foot, when Griffin was upon her, kneeling behind her and touching her in all the places he'd missed so far. Sarah sighed at the sensations coursing through her body, feeling more wanted and cherished than she'd ever felt in her life. And loved, she realized with no small amount of wonder. Griffin made her feel that, too.

She turned on the bed to face him, both still kneeling, circling an arm around his neck to pull him down for a kiss. As he drew nearer, he pushed her backward, until she was flat on her back and he was lying atop her, bracing himself on his strong forearms. She hooked her legs over his, curling her fingers over his taut thighs, and silently bade him to enter her welcoming warmth. He needed no further encouragement. With a single, fierce thrust he was inside her, and both cried out at the perfect consonance of their union.

Deeper and deeper Griffin ventured inside her, reaching places in Sarah that had never been touched before. He bent near her ear to murmur erotic promises, then carried them out, one by exhausting one. For what seemed like days, he gave her pleasure, the rectangle of light on the bed growing longer and dimmer as the time passed. Finally he came to her one last time, burying himself completely inside to rocket them both over the top.

What had begun as a fast, demanding need ultimately ended in a slow, languid satisfaction. Sarah and Griffin lay still and silent for a long time, each too overwhelmed to break what fragile hold they held on the afternoon's encounter, each too frightened by the tenuous fragility of their newfound intimacy to risk spoiling it by saying the wrong thing.

As Sarah lay nestled against Griffin, she marveled at what stroke of luck must have thrown this man into her path. She grinned when she recalled that she had originally considered their first meeting anything but fortuitous. Had someone told her then that she would wind up falling madly in love with the infuriating Officer Lawless, she would have laughed out loud. Now, however, all she could do was smile.

There was a question she wanted to ask him but was completely uncertain how to approach it. She twined her fingers in the dark hair swirling about his chest, then decided it might be best simply to be straightforward. "Griffin?" she asked softly, her voice sounding muted and mellow in the warm, close air of the bedroom.

"Hmm?"

"Did you mean what you said a little while ago?"

She felt him stir beside her, felt his arm tighten to keep her close. "Did I mean what?" he asked.

She took a deep breath, voicing her next words as she quickly exhaled. "Did you mean it when you said you loved me?"

Sarah felt more than heard him gasp, and wished immediately that she could take back her question. But before she had the chance to try, Griffin responded.

"Yes," he said. "Yes, I meant it."

She squirmed beside him until she was able to see his face completely. He looked tired and uneasy, and not a little scared. She cupped her hand over his rough jaw and grinned.

"Really?" she asked.

He nodded slowly. "Really."

"Then say it again."

"I love you, Sarah," he replied immediately.

She snuggled back against him, feeling a new, different kind of heat seep into her body. "I love you, too, Griffin," she said softly. "I love you, too."

Her quietly uttered words were almost Griffin's undoing. How the hell was he supposed to tell her about her brother now? *I love you, Sarah. Oh, and by the way, I'm arresting your brother this evening. I kind of neglected to mention that I've been investigating him virtually since the day you and I met. He'll be spending the next few years in the state pen because of me, and you'll only be able to see him on visiting days. He'll lose a number of the basic rights you and I enjoy, and his life will never be the same again, as a direct result of my activities. Just thought you'd like to know.* Yeah, that was sure to keep her right here by his side.

Griffin sighed, opened his mouth to say something, quickly changed his mind and snapped it shut again. How had he managed to get himself into this? he wondered. Of all the lousy luck.

"What time is it?" Sarah asked sleepily beside him.

Automatically he glanced at his wrist, only to find it watchless, then looked around, uncertain what had happened to the timepiece during their lovemaking.

"I think I put it on the nightstand after I removed it," she said, evidently reading his mind.

But it wasn't there, either. He leaned over the side of the bed and saw his watch winking up at him from the floor. Reaching for it, he chuckled and said, "I guess you kicked it off when your foot went flying while I was—"

"Oh, yeah," she interrupted him, blushing furiously. "Now I remember. I think I broke that bud vase, too. But don't worry," she added quickly. "It was strictly cheap carnival glass. Those pieces are a dime a dozen."

He laughed. "I don't care if it was worth half a million," he said. "It was worth it to have you—"

"Griffin..." she groaned, silently begging him not to bring up their recent sexual gymnastics. "Just tell me what time it is."

His grin turned to a frown when he saw the time. "You're not going to like it."

"Why not?"

"It's after six."

"Omigosh," Sarah gasped as she jumped up from the bed. Hastily she circled the room and began to gather her clothing, trying to put it on as she hurried about. "Mrs. MacAfee's going to kill me for being late again. I wouldn't blame her if she quit. Do you know how hard it is to find a decent sitter? It's next to impossible. It took me months to find her. All the other applicants had names like Charlie Manson or Betty Mussolini. Or they looked like they'd just caught the last boat off the Island of Dr. Moreau."

"Sarah, you can't leave yet," Griffin told her. "There's something we have to talk about."

She finished buttoning her blouse, looked down to see that she had skipped a button somewhere along the line, then rapidly began to unbutton it again. "I can't," she said as she completed the task once more, this time with greater success. "I really have to go."

"But, Sarah—"

"Why don't you come home and have dinner with me and the boys?" she asked as she haphazardly stuffed her blouse into her skirt and zipped it up. "We can talk afterward."

He shook his head. "I can't. I have to meet Stony in about half an hour."

"Well, Stony could come, too. We can invite Elaine and Jonah."

"No, that's impossible," Griffin told her. "Stony and I have to make an arrest tonight."

Sarah's head snapped up and she grinned at him. "Oh, that sounds so exciting. Bagging some crook to make society safer for innocent folks like me."

He seized upon her words. "Yes!" he exclaimed, sitting up straighter in bed. When the sheet dipped low around his hips, and Sarah's expression grew speculative, he clutched it behind him like a toga. "That's right," he went on quickly, hoping he sounded more effective as a law-enforcement officer than he felt at the moment. "That's why I'm going after this guy. Because he's a crook and has forfeited his right to be a member of the law-abiding community. And don't you forget it."

Sarah leaned forward and kissed him briefly on the lips. "And I love you for it," she said before turning to leave.

"Sarah!" he called after her.

At the bedroom door she turned, her face a silent question mark. He opened his mouth to say so many things that needed to be said, but was suddenly overcome by a sense of helplessness that almost crippled him. "I love you, too," he said softly, knowing it probably wouldn't be enough.

She smiled at him, a beautiful, happy, carefree smile, then lifted her fingers to her lips, blew him a kiss and was gone. Griffin wished he could feel as uninhibited and unencumbered as Sarah must feel right now. But all he could think about was what the night ahead of him held. All he could do was envision Sarah's face the next time he saw her, knowing it would hold none of the qualities she'd shown him only moments ago. The next time he would see hurt, betrayal and anger. And all of it would be because of him.

He heard the front door downstairs close behind her, and it seemed such a sad, conclusive sound. Throwing the bed-clothes aside, he rose to dress, but without the hasty excitement of his companion. Griffin was in no hurry to get where he needed to be. He only wished the night ahead of him was over. Over so he could get back to living his life the way he'd lived it before all this had begun—alone. Funny how it hadn't occurred to him before to be lonely in his solitary existence. But now that he'd have memories of Sarah Greenleaf to haunt him, loneliness would be a necessary side effect.

He couldn't let her go, he told himself. No matter what happened after tonight, he had to hang on to her. She might be Wallace Greenleaf's sister, but she was Griffin Lawless's love. And through whatever means necessary, legal or not, he would see to it she remained in his life forever.

Ten

Later that night, just as Sarah was finishing up the dinner dishes, the telephone rang. Certain it was Griffin, she yelled to her sons to turn down the television in the living room and reached for the receiver, murmuring a quick hello.

"Sarah, I've been arrested."

She gripped the phone more steadily in one hand, trying with the other to shift the plate she was washing under the stream of rinse water. "Wally?" she asked. "Is that you? What did you say?"

"I've been arrested," her brother repeated from the other end of the line, his voice sounding distant and tinny, carrying none of the swaggering confidence it normally displayed.

"*What?*" she exclaimed, dropping the plate back into the soapy water. He had her full attention now. "Arrested? What for?"

"My attorney is in Grand Cayman until the end of the week," he went on without clarifying. "You're going to have to come down here and bail me out."

"Bail you out?" she echoed, still unable to believe what her brother was telling her. "Why? What are the charges?"

"Trumped up," he was quick to reply. "Look, it's all some mix-up, I assure you. And it will all be straightened out soon enough. Then I'm going to sue the hell out of the Clemente P.D. for false arrest and take a nice long vacation in Tahiti on the proceeds. When can you get here?"

Sarah shook her head, trying to clear out the cobwebs. "I don't know. I mean, how much money do I need to bring?"

"Well, they've set my bail at fifty thousand dollars—"

"Fifty thousand dollars!"

"But you only need to have ten percent of that."

"Five thousand dollars?" she gasped, amazed that she'd been able to perform even that simple mathematical task.

"Yeah, so how long before you can get down here with it?"

She *might* be able to scrape up fifty bucks, Sarah thought, trying to remember what the balance in her checking account was. But five thousand? Who did her brother think she was? Nelson Rockefeller? "Wally, I don't have five thousand dollars."

"What do you mean, you don't have it?"

His proprietary, self-important tone of voice came back with a vengeance then, raising Sarah's hackles with its arrival. "I don't have five thousand dollars," she repeated, speaking slowly, as if to a toddler. "I'm not made of money, you know."

"Come on, it's just five gees. You mean to tell me you don't even have access to that amount of money?"

"Of course not."

Wally was quiet for a moment, then said, "They'll take deeds to property. You own your house, right? You got it in the divorce. Just sign that over to them."

"Wallace Greenleaf, you are out of your mind if you think I'm going to put my house on the line for bail money. You haven't even told me what you're under arrest for."

"I'm good for the money, Sarah. You know I am."

Sarah was torn. She wanted to help her brother, but how on earth was she supposed to do that without the means? "Why don't you call Mom?" she suggested. "She's all fired up to invest in your projects. She must have that kind of money she could wire down to you."

"Not since she invested in the cafeteria," Wally told her.

"You took Mom's last dollar to invest in that crazy scheme of yours?"

"It wasn't exactly her *last* dollar," he said. "And besides, the turnover on that cafeteria will be enormous. You should throw some of your own cash into the pot."

"Yeah, well, like I said, Wally, I don't have any to spare."

Something was wrong here, Sarah thought. Her brother might be many things, but she couldn't imagine a single one of them being something for which he would be placed under arrest. As much as she sometimes wished it were, being a persistent jerk wasn't illegal. So why was Wally so resistant to telling her exactly what the charges were?

"Tell me what you've been arrested for," she said. "And then I'll decide whether or not I'll put my house at risk."

"Sarah..."

"Wally..." she mimicked in his petulant tone.

He sighed, a loud, exasperated sound that was even more annoying thanks to the phone's distortion of it. "Bait advertising," he finally told her.

Sarah frowned. "Bait advertising? I've never heard of that. What is it? It doesn't sound so bad. It sounds like a misdemeanor."

"It is."

"They set your bail at fifty thousand dollars for a single misdemeanor?"

He sighed again, an even more exasperated sound this time, and continued, "They've also charged me with deceptive business practices and commercial bribery."

Sarah's stomach clenched into a knot. "Those charges sound more serious."

"They're still misdemeanors," Wally told her. "Just as most of the other charges are."

"*Most* of the *other* charges?" she parroted. She was getting tired of her brother's games. "Wally, just spit it out, will you?"

"All right, all right. I've been charged with thirty-seven misdemeanor counts."

"Oh, Wally."

"But nothing that's going to stick," he was quick to add.

"What's the big one they got you for?" she asked him, more than a little afraid to discover what it would be.

He paused for a long moment before replying. "Bribery of a public servant," he finally said. "A felony. Class *D*. Fourteen counts."

"Oh, Wally," she repeated miserably.

"But I've been framed, Sarah," he assured her. "I swear I have. You know me. I am *not* a crook."

Sarah shook her head slowly. Frankly, she didn't know what to believe. Her brother had done some dumb things in his life, and she honestly wouldn't be surprised to discover he was still at it. But bribery? Of a public servant, no less? Something that was clearly a major legal no-no? Was he truly capable of committing such a crime? Was he really that stupid?

This time it was Sarah who sighed, a long, weary, expulsion of breath. She ran a hand through her hair and thought for a moment. Immediately Griffin came to mind, and she smiled. He was a cop. He'd know what to do. He could help her out.

"Look," she told Wally, "let me call Griffin and see—"

"Who?"

"Griffin," she repeated. "Griffin Lawless. He's that, uh . . . friend of mine you met at the house a few weeks ago. He's a cop, and maybe he can—"

"Oh, man, I *knew* that guy looked familiar."

"What?"

"I got news for you, little sister. One of the cops who arrested me was your pal."

"*What?*"

"Yeah, the whole time he was reading me my rights and handcuffing me—"

"He, uh, he handcuffed you?" Sarah interrupted, assuring herself that her interest was only idle curiosity. Then she quickly chastised herself for forgetting the seriousness of the situation at hand. She adopted a more outraged tone as she clarified, "I mean, he *handcuffed* you? How despicable."

"Yeah," Wally went on, evidently not noticing her slip. "And the whole time he was doing it, I kept telling him, 'You look awfully familiar. Have we met?' And he just ignored me."

"Are you sure it was Griffin?" she asked. "Griffin Lawless?"

"Positive. In fact, I remember saying something about how ironic it was, him being a cop named Lawless and all."

Oh, and he'd probably loved that, Sarah thought. He'd probably thrown Wally that same perturbed expression he'd given her on their initial meeting when she'd made the same observation. Then she immediately remembered that the man she was recalling so affectionately, the man with whom she'd made love only hours ago, the man she'd said she loved and who claimed to love her back, had just arrested her brother. He had told her outright that afternoon that he was making an arrest tonight, but had conveniently neglected to mention that the arrestee was none other than her brother, Wally. A brother he'd met in her kitchen less than two weeks ago, she reminded herself further. A man there was no mistaking was a member of her family.

Griffin Lawless had lied to her.

The realization hit Sarah in the head as if someone had smacked her. Before arresting someone, a cop had to investigate that person, right? She'd learned that much from television shows. So Griffin must have been investigating Wally for some time. How long, she had no idea. But she couldn't help wondering if the beginning of his interest in Wally's activities coincided directly with his interest in her life. Was that why he'd gotten close to her in the first place? Because she was Wally's sister and he wanted to use her to uncover more about her brother's life?

No, that couldn't be, she decided. She couldn't remember a single time when he'd even mentioned Wally's name around her, let alone asked her any questions about him, other than the normal, curious, personal ones that arose whenever the two of them were discussing their families. If he'd wanted to know more about Wally's professional life, he would have asked.

Another, more troubling thought struck her. Was she, too, under suspicion of some kind? Was that why Griffin had insinuated himself into her life? Was he hoping to uncover something illegal about her, as well? He had ticketed her for speeding, after all. In his eyes, that probably indicated she had a congenital propensity for breaking the law. Naturally he would be suspicious of her, she thought. But did the police actually carry their investigations so far that they wound up in the suspect's bed?

"Sarah? Are you still there?"

She shook her head to clear it and replied with some distraction. "Yes, Wally, I'm still here."

"So now that *your* cop pal has hauled my butt down to jail, what are *you* going to do about it?"

Wally's demanding, reproachful voice, so clearly condemning her for something he'd gotten himself into, set Sarah's teeth on edge. That did it. She'd had it. Had it with brothers, had it with cops, had it with men. She'd go down to the police station and see what—if anything—she could do to expedite Wally's release. And while she was there, maybe she'd look around for Griffin, because she had more than a few questions for him. And if Wally insisted on behaving like a child, and if Griffin's responses didn't meet with her satisfaction, she fully intended to wash her hands of both of them.

Griffin had a headache. A mind-numbing, earsplitting, shoulder-tensing migraine that had come upon him the moment he'd rapped his knuckles against Wallace Greenleaf's front door. One that simply would not go away. He swallowed a fourth aspirin—knowing the tablet would probably do little more than eat a hole in his stomach lining—propped his elbows on his desk and cradled his head in his hands. If bad days were wild horses, he thought, he had just been stampeded into mush.

"I'd like to have a word with you."

It was a voice he'd been expecting to hear all night, but one he had dreaded nonetheless. He dropped his hands to his desk, glanced up to find Sarah glaring back at him and tried to smile.

"Hi," he said. "Is there a problem, Ms. Greenleaf?"

She was wearing those tight, short cutoffs that had nearly driven him mad at the softball game and a loose-fitting, purple T-shirt that read My Mom Went To Atlantic City and All I Got Was This Lousy T-shirt. Her hair was a mess, her face devoid of all makeup, and she was angry. Very, very angry by the looks of it. Griffin didn't think he'd ever wanted anything more than to pull her into his arms and kiss her senseless that instant. But he looked beyond her to see that Jack and Sam were seated with uncharacteristic quiet on a bench behind her—safely out of earshot—watching intently every move he and Sarah made. So instead he cupped his hands behind his head, leaned back in his chair and waited for her to tear him apart.

"You lied to me," she said without preamble.

"No, I didn't."

She tugged the strap of her purse more forcefully over her shoulder, leaving her fingers curled around the length of leather. He wasn't sure if she was fearful of having her purse snatched by some questionable lowlife in the police station, or if she simply felt the need to have something—even something as slender and nonthreatening as her arm—creating a barrier in front of her.

"Yes, you did, too," she insisted.

"I'm sorry, Sarah," he began again. "But I beg to differ. I never lied to you."

"How long had you been investigating Wally before you arrested him?" she demanded.

"About six weeks, but—"

"Right around the time you started sniffing around my front door," she interrupted. "I'd say that gave you ample opportunity to tell me you were investigating my brother."

"I'm not at liberty to divulge the specifics of an ongoing investigation to laypeople," Griffin said, wishing at the last moment that he'd chosen another word besides *laypeople* to indicate Sarah. It was an impossibly inappropriate gaffe, one she'd evidently noted, because a red flush that had nothing to do with embarrassment crept up her throat and darkened her cheeks.

"Yeah, and I guess that's all I was to you, wasn't I?"

Griffin rose from his chair with enough force to send it toppling backward. Sarah flinched, but did not move away from him. If anything, her posture became more challenging. She settled her hands on her hips in the ages-old gesture of defiance.

"That's not true and you know it," he snapped, somehow managing to keep his voice low. He had already noted that the two of them were generating much interest among both her sons and the other detectives in the squad room. "I entered the investigation into your brother's activities long after it had begun."

"But you knew Wally was my brother. You knew you were..." She paused, dropping her gaze to the floor, suddenly unable to meet his gaze. Her voice, too, was quieter when she spoke again. "You knew you were getting involved with the sister of one of your suspects, but you did nothing to stop that involvement. To me, that smacks of unethical behavior if nothing else. Although I myself have a few other words I could call it."

Griffin knew he shouldn't ask, but couldn't help himself. "Such as?"

She jerked her head up again and studied him levelly. "Such as lowdown, sneaky, calculating, self-serving, cold-hearted—"

"All right, all right. I get the gist of it." He rubbed at a knot in his neck and sighed. "Look. I'm no more thrilled about how this all turned out than you are. But the fact is, your brother is a criminal who's landed himself in a lot of trouble. I had nothing to do with that, Sarah. I'm just the guy they assigned to bring him in."

She stared at him for a long time without speaking, and he could tell she was thinking hard about something. "This isn't about Wally," she finally said.

He arched his left brow skeptically. "No?"

She shook her head. "No, not entirely. This is about the fact that you lied to me. That you were investigating him while you were sleeping with me." She held up a hand to stop his protest before he could utter it. "Because you'll never convince me there was anything more to your feelings for me than wanting sex. If there had been, you would have been honest with me. Maybe not from the start, I'll grant you that. But the least you could have done, Griffin, was warn me about what was going to happen."

"And risk you tipping off your brother before we could arrest him?"

"I wouldn't have done that!"

"Wouldn't you?"

Sarah started to immediately deny Griffin's allegation, then paused to give the question more thorough consideration before replying. She had come down to the police station full of fire and indignation, ready to nail him to the wall for what he'd done. She'd been mad about her brother's arrest, and madder still about the fact that Griffin had known all along what was going to happen and hadn't even clued her in. She'd been mad that he had gotten involved with her while he was investigating Wally. But right now, she wasn't sure what made her maddest of all.

"Why couldn't you have just waited?" she asked him softly. "Why couldn't you have just gone about your business, done whatever it was you were obligated by your job to do, then called me to ask me out when it was all over?"

"Oh, right," Griffin replied sarcastically. "Like you really would have gone out with the man who'd tossed your brother's keester into the can."

She lifted a hand to her forehead, rubbing vigorously to dispel an ache that throbbed between her eyes. She was hurt, confused and angry, and she had no idea what to think. "Was it really that important to you?" she asked. "That I go out with you?"

"Yes," he responded immediately. "It was that important. You've become more important to me than anything else in my life ever has."

She sighed, suddenly feeling more exhausted than she could ever recall feeling. "Oh, Griffin. You've ruined everything."

He came around the front of his desk, curved his palms possessively over her shoulders and held her until she looked up to meet his gaze. What she saw in his eyes made her stomach clench into a knot. His reaction to the situation mirrored her own, she realized. But he was less willing to give up hope than she was.

"How on earth have *I* ruined everything?" he asked.

"Well, obviously there's going to be a trial now," she said.

"Yes."

"A trial that will put you and Wally on opposite sides of the fence."

"Yes."

"You'll be doing your damnedest to put him behind bars, and he'll be fighting for his life. Because no matter what happens with this thing, Griffin, his life will never be the same after it's all over."

"So what's your point, Sarah?"

"Don't you see?" she pleaded with him. "Maybe I haven't always seen eye to eye with my brother. Hell, I don't know if I've ever seen eye to eye with him. And even if he's guilty of what you say he is..." She lifted a hand into the air as if groping for help, doubled her hand into a fist, then dropped it helplessly back to her side. "He's still my brother," she finished softly. "And he's always been a part of my life. He always will be."

"And I won't." Griffin spoke aloud what she had left unsaid.

"I don't know if you will be or not," Sarah told him honestly.

"So it is about Wally, after all."

"No, Griffin, it's about us."

He shook his head silently, and she could tell he didn't understand.

"I won't be able to see you for a while," she said, shrugging his hands off her shoulders and taking a step backward. "Not during the trial. This will be difficult enough to go through without the added burden of... of sorting out my love life."

"Sarah, don't do this," he pleaded. "Don't just throw away what you and I have together."

"As it stands right now, we have nothing except a couple of great sexual encounters that were based on deception."

He shook his head. "No, what we have is a love for each other like very few people ever know."

"You can't have love without trust, Griffin," she was quick to point out. "And you can't have trust where there's been deception."

"I swear to you, Sarah, I never meant to—"

"But you did anyway," she interrupted him. "Didn't you?"

Griffin looked at Sarah, looked at the two boys seated so still and so clearly worried behind her. With the three of them, he had begun to think he might find something he'd thought he would never have. He had hoped he'd finally found a family. He didn't know what he could say or do that would change Sarah's mind. He tried to put himself in her place, tried to sympathize with how she must feel. But all he could see was his future slipping away from him, a future he hadn't until that moment realized meant more to him than anything in the world.

"What can I do?" he asked her desperately. "What can I say that will make everything the way it was?"

But Sarah only shook her head silently. "It will never be the way it was. Never again." She took another step backward. "Now I have to go see about getting my brother out of jail. Don't try to contact me, Griffin. I need some time. A lot of time."

"But when will I see you again?" He took a step after her, hesitating only when she turned around to face him again.

She lifted her fingers to her brow. It was furrowed in worry, and if he didn't know her better, he would swear Sarah Greenleaf was about to burst into tears.

"I don't know," she told him softly. "I just don't know."

"What you and I had, Sarah," he began, lowering his voice to a near whisper, "it wasn't just sleeping together." He tried to ignore the fact that he had just used the past tense in referring to the two of them. But apparently his slip didn't pass by Sarah.

"What we *had* is right, Griffin. Now we have nothing. And as far as what the future might offer us . . ."

She shrugged, a gesture he found unbearable to watch. It suggested that she was willing to just let it all go, that she would give it all up without a fight.

And with that she spun around again, gathered her sons with one arm around each of them and hurried out of the squad room. Griffin watched the double doors swing back and forth a dozen times, until they finally stilled completely. All around him phones were ringing, typewriters were clacking, computers were beeping and people were shouting. The squad room was busy for a weekday night. But Griffin had never felt more alone.

Eleven

The trial two months later was actually much less eventful and dramatic than Sarah had anticipated it would be, and nothing at all like those Matlock movies on television. The lawyers involved were rather bland-looking, long-winded men who seemed to go on and on about nothing at all. They spoke a lot of legalese she couldn't begin to understand, and even more confusing business and corporate mumbo jumbo.

Wally never had spelled out for her precisely what the charges against him involved or how they had come to be pressed in the first place. Instead he had used most of his breath complaining about how honest, hardworking men went to prison while the streets were rife with the lowest form of riffraff that no one bothered to bring to justice. In reply, Sarah had agreed that the justice system was indeed in a sorry state—as was her bank account—and had told Wally that unfortunately he was just going to have to stay in jail until his lawyer returned from his vacation and could get him out.

And now as she sat in the courtroom studying the back of her brother's head, she still had no idea what was going on. She knew only that Griffin Lawless had shown up about fifteen minutes ago, and it had taken all the energy she possessed to keep her eyes from straying to the other side of the room where he sat. She had automatically glanced over her shoulder at the sound of the courtroom door opening behind her, only to find her gaze fixed with his. He was wearing a dove gray lightweight suit unlike anything she'd ever seen him wear, his blue eyes seeming even paler matched with the light color.

For a moment that seemed to stretch to eternity, they had studied each other, until Sarah had finally forced herself to look away. She fiddled with the buttons dotting the front of her gold suit jacket and tried to forget she'd seen him. But every scrape of his shoes against the floor as he'd walked toward his seat had resounded in her ears like a thunderclap. And she was positive she somehow managed to pick up his scent, even from such a distance. Of course, she knew she was crazy. She hadn't seen him for more than two months. She wasn't sure she even remembered how he smelled.

Oh, who was she kidding? Sarah demanded of herself. She could remember every inch of Griffin Lawless's body, every sound he'd ever made, every word he'd ever spoken. The man had haunted her everywhere she went. Her house was full of memories of him. Even driving in her car afforded her no escape. She constantly found herself glancing into the rearview mirror, hoping he would appear behind her on his motorcycle, as if she could rewind the past few months and start all over with him again.

She wished he had at least *tried* to contact her since their last parting.

The air in the courtroom suddenly felt very hot and confining, and Sarah rose to exit as silently and unobtrusively as possible. Outside in the wide corridor, the hustle and bustle of people stirred the cooler air around her, and she welcomed the change of scenery. She relaxed for a moment—until she felt the presence of someone standing behind her. Without turning around, she knew it was Griffin. And when she made no move to acknowledge him, he walked around to stand in front of her.

"I won't go away just because you ignore me," he told her.

She met his gaze, scrambling for something light, breezy and indifferent to say. Unfortunately, light, breezy and indifferent was in no way how she felt at the moment.

"And I won't go away just because you tell me to, either," he added quickly, as if fearful that such a statement would be the first words out of her mouth.

"Hello, Griffin," she finally said, resigned to the fact that she was going to have to speak to him sooner or later. "How have you been?"

Her question seemed to rankle him, because he frowned at her. "How the hell do you think I've been? Do you even really care?"

She wanted to shout, Yes! Of course she cared! That not a night passed when she didn't lay in her bed, staring at the pillow beside her, wondering what he was doing elsewhere and with whom. She wanted to tell him how frequently the boys asked about him, how their enthusiasm for nearly everything had diminished significantly since Griffin had disappeared from their lives.

She wanted to tell him how much she missed him. How much she loved him.

But instead she only said, "I hope you've been well."

One side of his mouth lifted in a sarcastic twist. "Yeah, I'll just bet you do."

Sarah had no desire to stand around sniping. If these were to be the last words they spoke to each other—and she feared terribly that such might just be the case—then she didn't want to waste time arguing. "Was there something you wanted, Griffin?"

He laughed, a completely humorless sound. "Want?" he repeated lasciviously. "Oh, yeah. There are one or two things I *want*. But nothing that can be described in polite society."

She flattened her mouth into a thin line. How could he reduce what they'd had to nothing more than the sexual? she wondered morosely. Maybe, she then answered herself reluctantly, because that's exactly what she had done the last time she'd seen him.

Unhappy with her realization and anxious to remove herself from an uncomfortable situation, she said, "Then if there's nothing else...?" She started to turn, searching for a suitable escape route, wondering where the nearest women's room was. If she didn't get out of there soon, she was going to do something really stupid. Like cry. Or throw herself into his arms and make him promise never to leave her again.

"You haven't been to the house in weeks," he said, his words no longer cool and swaggering but edged with a longing and wistfulness that tore at Sarah's heart. "Every time I stop by, Elaine is there, instead."

She hesitated in her retreat, meeting his gaze once again. Her voice was quiet when she spoke, free of the sharpness and accusation she wished she could feel. "Under the circumstances, we thought it might be better if she took over the appraisal for a while. After she's done with the furnishings and jewelry, I'll come back and finish up the rest. Don't worry," she found herself adding. "I should be out of your hair before the end of the year."

"I don't want you out of my hair," Griffin said. "I want you to talk to me. To let me explain. Dammit, to listen to reason."

"There's nothing for us to talk about," she insisted.

"Oh, I think there's *plenty* for us to talk about," he countered.

"Griffin, I told you two months ago that I can't do this until after the trial."

"And two months ago I thought I could handle that. But I've changed my mind. I need to talk to you. Now."

She drew in a deep breath, gestured at an empty bench, then made her way toward it, assuming he would follow her.

Griffin took a moment to watch Sarah as she walked away from him, noting the subtle sway of her hips that her boxy gold jacket and straight skirt did nothing to hide. He smiled as he followed her to the bench. Sarah Greenleaf sure had some way of walking—confident, self-assured, unwilling to be messed with. Just this once, he wished she'd feel some niggling sense of uncertainty. Just enough to put them on equal footing, since he was beginning to feel anything but sure of himself.

He took his seat beside her, deliberately leaving a solid six or eight inches between them so that she wouldn't feel threatened. But he couldn't keep himself from stretching an arm along the back of the bench behind her. He would just have to find the strength somehow to keep his fingers from tangling in her hair and pulling her head close to his so that he could kiss her. That shouldn't be so tough, should it? he thought. Surely a man with as much self-control as he possessed could be trusted to behave himself, right?

"I can't stop thinking about you," he blurted out before he could stop himself, grimacing at the tone of desperation he knew he hadn't been able to disguise. He was sure he had planned to start this conversation in an entirely different manner, but somehow he had wound up uttering the first thing that had come into his head. Nonetheless, he continued frankly, "I miss you, Sarah. And I want you back in my life."

She sighed deeply, closing her eyes as she tipped her head back and leaned it against the wall. "Well, we can't always have what we want, can we? If we could, I'd have hair like Cindy Crawford's, and I'd be sitting on a beach in Saint-Tropez, sipping a pĩna colada while some young stud who spoke not a word of English fanned me with a palm frond."

Griffin couldn't help but smile. "Well, I could take you to the pool at the Y, buy you a Dreamsicle and try to remember my high school Spanish, if that would help. As long as you don't mind me whispering sweet nothings like 'Juan is at the library' into your ear. And I could fan you with the latest issue of *Sports Illustrated*. Frankly, I think your hair is perfect."

He saw Sarah fighting a smile, but she didn't look at him. Still, it was a good sign.

"Why do you have to be so nice and wonderful, when I'm doing my best to hate you?" she asked.

Griffin shook his head, reaching over to wind a blond curl around his finger. "Just my nature, I guess."

She opened her eyes and studied him then, but didn't pull away. "There's something that's been bothering me all along about all this," she said.

"Just one thing?" he asked. There had been a lot of things bothering him about it. "What's that?"

"If it was so important to you to ask me out, that I be a part of your life, then why didn't you request that you be removed from the case they were building against Wally? You could have still kept the information from me, but at least I would have known you tried not to compromise our relationship."

"I did put in a request to be transferred to another case," Griffin told her.

She lifted her brows in surprise, sitting up straighter in her seat. "You did?"

He nodded. "But there was no one else who could take it. The department is shorthanded to begin with, and everyone was overloaded with cases. Plus this was my first case—I was low man on the totem pole. I couldn't very well refuse."

"And Stony knew all along, too, that Wally was my brother?"

Griffin shook his head. "No, he didn't. No offense, Sarah, but he couldn't even remember your last name after he met you the first time. He knew you only as Elaine's friend, Sarah, and as my, uh, my girlfriend, I guess. I never made the connection for him.''

''Why not?''

He shrugged. ''I guess I didn't want him to think I was a creep, either. Investigating the brother of the woman I was involved with.''

''Then why did you get involved with me?'' she asked him again.

He fixed his gaze on hers as he said softly, ''I couldn't resist you, Sarah. From the moment I laid eyes on you, I couldn't stop thinking about you. You got under my skin the minute I saw your face. And when you asked, 'Is there a problem, Officer?' I wanted to drag you out of the car, kiss you until we both couldn't see straight and say, 'Yeah, a big problem. Now, what are we going to do about it?' ''

She watched him in silence for a long time. He wished he could tell what she was thinking, wished there were some way to know exactly how she felt. ''I love you, Sarah,'' he said, uncertain when he'd decided to speak. ''And I don't know what I'll do without you.''

Her eyes betrayed her then. One minute they were studying him with frank assessment and the next they were filled with tears. She still loved him, too, he thought as he lifted a finger to trace the delicate line of her cheekbone. He could feel it as surely as he could feel the soft warmth of her skin beneath his fingertip. So why didn't she say it out loud?

''You're still thinking about your brother,'' he said, dropping his hand back to his lap. ''You're still thinking you should be loyal to him.''

Sarah dropped her gaze to the fingers twisting nervously together in her lap. ''I don't know what to do, Griffin. Even if he's guilty of the crimes you say, he's still my brother. My family. I never really thought much about that before I met you, but I guess the ties that bind us by blood are stronger than I thought.''

''Even stronger than the ties that bind us by love?''

She didn't answer one way or the other, something Griffin tried to tell himself was an encouraging sign. Nonetheless, they were no closer to a resolution to their problem now than they had been two months ago. He closed his eyes and pinched the bridge of his nose in an effort to ease the throbbing between his temples. Man, he'd been getting a lot of headaches lately.

"Griffin?"

When he opened his eyes again, it was to find Sarah staring at him intently. "Yes?" he replied.

"Tell me exactly what it is Wally did that was so wrong."

He looked at her curiously. "Hasn't he already told you about the charges?"

She shook her head. "Not really. I mean, he's told me what they are, but he never really said what he did that got him into trouble in the first place."

Griffin sighed deeply. Where should he begin? How did one politely tell a woman that her own brother was a liar and a cheat and a thief? "Well," he began, "what Wally and Jerry did was encourage people to invest in schemes of theirs that they knew from the beginning would never materialize. They took thousands of dollars from people—usually elderly people who were easy targets, or people living off their savings who were in desperate need of a financial jolt—assuring them that the project Jerwal was developing would give them a fast return for their investment that would exceed their wildest dreams.

"They told the investors their money was being used to acquire land and rent equipment, when in fact the cash was just being socked into a bank in the Bahamas. Then your brother and his partner bribed local government officials to sign phony documents that would legally prohibit the construction of whatever they claimed to be building. Which gave them the means to tell the investors that the project had been forced down for legal reasons completely beyond their control, and that the investments had gone bust through no fault of Jerwal's. It was an obvious case of fraud, Sarah. They had a clear intent to swindle people from the outset."

Sarah listened to Griffin's account of Wally's activities, wishing with all her heart that she could rush to her brother's defense with righteous indignation. Unfortunately she couldn't quite convince herself that Wally hadn't done what Griffin said he had. Her brother *was* ambitious. And he *did* have a very intense desire to get rich quick. What Griffin described was, sadly, not beyond the realm of possibility.

"What kind of schemes?" she asked softly.

"What?"

Sarah tried to speak a little more loudly. "What kind of schemes did Wally and Jerry get people to invest in?"

"Well, when we nailed them, they had two major ones in the works. One was some roller-blade rink and another was—if you can believe this—a topless cafeteria."

Sarah's head snapped up at that. She looked over at Griffin, but he was looking away.

"I mean, can you imagine people actually putting up good money for such a thing?" he went on before she could speak. "Sometimes I think people who are conned over something that stupid deserve to be fleeced."

"This topless cafeteria," Sarah said, "are you sure it was a scam?"

Griffin looked at her curiously. "Absolutely. They'd collected hundreds of thousands of dollars from investors, and had books phonied up to make it look like they had already begun construction. But there was nothing concrete—no land, no equipment, no building. It was definitely a scam. We have proof. Why?"

Sarah shook her head and emitted a single, humorless chuckle. "Because my brother Wally convinced my mother to invest ten thousand dollars in that cafeteria," she said. "And he tried to get money from me, too."

"He asked his own sister and mother to invest in a phony project?"

She nodded. "I'll kill him."

"That won't be necessary," Griffin told her. "What he did isn't a capital offense. But he *is* going to jail—there's no question of that. And although it will be one of those minimum-security facilities, where he can learn to crochet and work on his backhand, he won't get out for a while."

"I can't believe he'd take his own mother like that," Sarah said, still unable to fathom what Griffin had told her. She'd known Wally could be a jerk, but this...this made him a world-class creep, too.

Family, Sarah repeated to herself with a rueful shake of her head. Oh, yeah. That was a tie that bound, all right. And to think she'd almost allowed it to ruin what was truly a vital bond to Griffin. She suddenly realized that there was more than blood involved in making a family. A lot more. There was loyalty and faith. There was trust and dependability. There was affection and absolution.

But most of all, there was love.

"Ah, Griffin?" she said quietly, scooting toward him until she had closed the small distance between them.

She could tell he was surprised by her sudden shift in posture, and she smiled encouragingly. "I just remembered that I left something at the Mercer house that I really need to get back. Could you, uh, could you by any chance give me a lift over there?"

He arched his brows in surprise. "Right now?"

She nodded. "Unless you have to stay and be a witness for the prosecution. Something, incidentally, that I'm thinking of becoming myself."

He smiled. "We wouldn't ask you to testify against your own brother."

She gritted her teeth at the door leading to the courtroom where Wally's trial was still in session. "I wouldn't mind. Honest."

Griffin chuckled. "We won't need you, I promise. And I'm not going to be called as a witness until tomorrow."

"Then you could take me home?" she asked. Quickly she clarified, "To your place, I mean."

He studied her for a moment before responding. "What exactly was it you left there that you need to get back right away?"

She smiled at him, curling her fingers around his neck, pulling his head toward hers. "My heart," she whispered before she kissed him softly on the mouth. "I left my heart there somewhere, and you have to help me find it."

"Here it is," Griffin said several hours later as he pressed his lips to the heated flesh between Sarah's breasts. He looked up at her and smiled. "I've found your heart, Sarah. Now, what do you want me to do with it?"

She smoothed back his damp hair and returned his smile. "Hold on to it," she said softly. "Keep it safe."

He straightened in bed until he lay beside her. The late-afternoon sun spilled through the window in what they had come to think of as Meredith's room, bathing them in a soft pale yellow that warmed Sarah's naked skin. She nuzzled closer to him, tucking her head into the hollow below his chin, opening her palm over his heart. The steady *thump-thump-thump* was a reassuring sensation, and she sighed. All her worry and fear of the past two months had evaporated the moment she and Griffin had come together, and now she was satisfied that nothing would ever come between them again. At least, she hoped not.

"Griffin?" she asked.

"Mmm?"

"What's going to happen now?"

He tilted his head until he was staring down at her, and she could see that he was puzzled. "What do you mean?"

"I mean with me, and you, and us, and this house and everything."

He lay back with his head resting on the pillow and stared at the ceiling. "You're still going to work on the house, right?"

She nodded.

"So I'm still your client?"

She nodded again, grinning. "Among other things."

His chest shook beneath her hand, rumbling with laughter. "So I am," he said.

"And us?" she said to encourage him further, feeling just a twinge of uncertainty. She had begun to assume that the two of them would be tangled up together like this for the rest of their lives. But she'd learned, thanks to her brother, that it was best not to assume anything. What if she'd been wrong about Griffin, too?

"Well," he began slowly, "I was kind of wondering what your sons would think if you and I moved in together."

Sarah frowned. Moved in together? she repeated to herself. That wasn't exactly what she'd had in mind. Not entirely, anyway. "They'd probably love it," she replied experimentally. "It would give them the run of their own house with no adult supervision."

"Well, naturally I was assuming that they would move in with us, too."

"Oh."

"So what do you think?"

"I, uh..." She what? Sarah thought. Oh, for pete's sake. she'd never been accused of hiding her feelings. Why didn't she just come right out and say what was on her mind? With a deep, fortifying breath, she quickly said, "Frankly, Griffin, I was rather hoping you'd ask me to marry you."

He turned on his side to look at her. "I thought I just did that."

She narrowed her eyes at him curiously. "No, you didn't. You just asked me to move in with you."

He made an exasperated sound. "Well, it's the same thing, isn't it?"

She chuckled. "Boy, you're a lot more old-fashioned than I thought."

"Look, will you marry me or not?" he demanded, clearly losing patience.

Sarah laughed harder. "Okay, okay. I'll marry you. Sheesh. I just hope you realize what you're getting yourself into. You'll not only get a wife, you'll get two kids, too."

He smiled and leaned down to kiss her. "Three for the price of one," he said. "Sounds like a real deal to me."

She kissed him back. "You'll soon discover that what you're calling a bargain will cost you a lot more than you think."

"Then we'll just have to make the expense worthwhile, won't we?"

His eyes fairly glowed with some unknown fire, as if he knew something she didn't. Sarah found herself growing warmer, but for the life of her didn't know why.

"What do you mean?" she asked.

He shook his head. "Nothing. Just that maybe we ought to add a couple more to the fold is all."

Her eyes widened at the thought. "You want to have more kids?"

He lifted his shoulder in a gesture she supposed was meant to be a shrug, yet seemed to her anything but careless. "Sure," he told her. "If you want to."

She smiled. "I do."

He smiled back. "I can't wait to hear you say those words to a minister."

She circled her arms around his neck, pulling him close again. "I can't wait to say them."

As he tucked her body in next to his, Griffin remembered that Sarah had asked him about the house, too. He knew she loved the old building, knew she'd hate to part with it. But he didn't think he could live here for the rest of his life. It was too big, too formal, too full of reminders of the family he'd never had. It simply wasn't a family dwelling.

"About the house, Sarah," he said, before they could lose themselves in passion again. "I don't want to live here."

He was surprised by her expression—one of profound relief.

"Oh, thank goodness," she whispered.

"You don't want to live here, either?"

"Oh, gosh, no," she assured him. "Can you imagine what Jack and Sam would do to this place?" A shudder wound through her body. "The antique community would never forgive me."

Griffin laughed, feeling relief wash over him, as well. "I was thinking about turning it into a museum," he said. "Donate the house and most of the furnishings and everything to the local historical society and let them worry about it. There are one or two things I wouldn't mind hanging on to—mostly Meredith's things—but for the most part, I'm just not comfortable in this place."

Sarah nodded her understanding. "Could there be just one stipulation in your agreement with the historical society?" she asked.

"Sure. What?"

"I'd like to play a part in overseeing the collection. If it's all right with you," she hastened to add. "I've become somewhat attached to the old place. It is, after all, what brought us together."

Griffin smiled. "You can play as big a part as you want," he told her. "But, Sarah, I have to disagree with you. This house isn't what brought us together."

"No?"

He shook his head, then leaned in close. "You breaking the law—that's what brought us together."

"*What?*" she said, outraged.

He laughed. "In fact, you're the most lawless woman I've ever known." He grinned lasciviously as he added, "And you know what we have to do with lawless women, don't you?"

She grinned back, evidently following his train of thought. "Lock them up?" she asked hopefully.

He nodded. "In handcuffs."

She sighed. "Oh, boy..."

Epilogue

Ah, spring. When a young man's fancy turned to thoughts of . . . softball. Griffin Lawless stretched languorously as he stepped out of the dugout. Although, he corrected himself, a man didn't have to be so young to be preoccupied by fancies. Nonetheless, for the past few months, he had been feeling like a kid again.

He lifted his arms over his head and pushed them backward, arching his back into the stretch. Then he selected a bat from the half-dozen or so leaning against the fence and took a few practice swings. Stony was about to strike out, and somebody was going to have to clean up his mess. Newlyweds, Griffin thought with a rueful shake of his head. They didn't know squat about how to play the game.

He looked toward the stands where Elaine, Jonah, Jack and Sam had raised their fists with index fingers extended, all of them shouting that the first precinct was number one. Then Griffin turned back to the dugout and smiled at the new coach. She was a cute little thing with her stubby blond ponytail and cap turned around backward. And the slight swell of her tummy rising over the life that had been growing inside her for the past five months only added to her charm. But she had a mouth on her...

"Strike!" she shouted at the umpire. "What do you mean 'strike?' I could see that was a ball all the way over here."

Sarah came stomping out of the dugout, brushed past Griffin and marched over to home plate. She wedged herself between Stony and the umpire, standing on tiptoe until she was nose to nose with the latter.

"I've gone up against better umps than you," she began, jabbing a finger against his ample stomach. "And I made mincemeat out of 'em. Now, you'd better get your act together, pal, or you'll be outta here faster than chili through a Chihuahua."

Griffin sighed and leaned on the bat. Might as well take a little break for a minute, he thought. This would go on for a while. He inhaled deeply, reveling in the aroma of freshly mown grass, corn dogs and dust. The hot sun beat down on his face, and arms, soothing sore muscles and easing his soul. He smiled. Life had never been this good before. And it only got better every day. He had a wife, two great kids and another on the way, and a life-style that pretty well guaranteed he'd be around for a long time to enjoy it.

No stress, he thought. No problems, no worries, no regrets. Never again. After the game, he and his family would go for pizza. Then they'd go home, to the two-story colonial they'd all chosen together last fall, and they'd spend the rest of their Saturday doing all the things families did together. It was a new way of life for Griffin, one he never wanted to see change.

Sarah came stomping back past him then, grumbling about why the umpire association would allow the admittance of lunatics. Griffin caught her in his arms before she could pass him and pulled her close. She made a half-hearted effort to brush his hands away, then snuggled close against him.

"Griffin," she murmured against his shoulder, "what will everyone say? They'll think I'm showing you favoritism."

He kissed her temple. "Well, aren't you?"

"Of course. But we don't want everyone else to know that."

"Why not?"

Sarah couldn't think of a very good answer, so she just shrugged and nestled even more closely into her husband's embrace, draping her arms around his waist. "I love you," she said softly.

He squeezed her briefly, then loosened his hold. "I love you, too."

"If you really loved me," she said with a smile, "you'd go out there and hit a homer."

She felt him chuckle, and her smile broadened.

"I'll see what I can do," he told her.

"Strike three!" the umpire called as Stony swung at air.

Sarah inhaled a deep breath to argue with the call, but Griffin halted her objection by pressing his mouth to hers. It was a brief kiss, but a thorough one. Enough to make her dizzy and lose her place in the scheme of things. The spectators erupted in applause, and Griffin went to take his turn at bat.

Sarah shook her head once to clear it, then turned her concentration to the pitch. It was low, inside, with just a bit of a curve, and her husband smacked the heck out of it. With a dull, but definite *thump*, the softball arced high into the air, gaining momentum as it rose until it soared out of sight over the fence. Griffin winked at her as he took off for first base.

Her heart hammered hard in her chest as he rounded third, and by the time he slapped his foot against home plate, she was running to meet him. She hurled herself against him, and he caught her to his chest, kissing her again.

"Gee, I guess you really do love me," she said breathlessly.

He nodded. "More than you could possibly know."

"Oh, I think I know," she assured him.

The rest of the team joined them in congratulations then, along with a few fans from the stands. There were still two innings to go, but Griffin had brought in two other runs with his, and now the first precinct claimed a substantial lead.

Sarah laughed as he spun her around one last time before setting her on her feet. "Way to go, Lawless," she said.

"Thanks, Coach."

They walked back to the dugout hand in hand, and fell onto the bench together. Hoping to find a candy bar, Sarah reached for Griffin's duffel bag, and heard a strange clinking sound inside. She smiled at him knowingly.

"You brought your handcuffs home from work again," she said.

He smiled back. "Well, the boys are staying with Jonah and the Stonestreets tonight, aren't they?"

She nodded.

"Well, then."

"Well, then," she repeated. She opened her palm over her softly protruding belly. "You remember what happened last time," she said. "I couldn't get to my diaphragm."

Griffin's hand splayed over hers. "Yeah. My plan worked perfectly."

She dropped her mouth open in surprise. "You planned that?"

"Naturally."

She was about to say more, but felt a flutter of something inside her. She laughed, and quickly reversed the positions of their hands. "There," she whispered. "Feel that? That's our daughter."

She watched Griffin's expression change from concentration to surprise to delight to awe. When his eyes met hers they were shinier than she'd ever seen them. "That's Meredith?" he asked.

Sarah nodded. "That's her."

She hooked her arm around his neck, pulling his head down beside hers, thinking this moment the most perfect she'd ever spent.

"This Meredith will be happy," Griffin said quietly.

Sarah nodded again. "I know. Just like her mother."

"And her father."

Neither paid much attention to the game after that. After all, Sarah conceded with a grin, there were one or two things more important than softball.

* * * * *

MILLION DOLLAR SWEEPSTAKES (III)

No purchase necessary. To enter, follow the directions published. Method of entry may vary. For eligibility, entries must be received no later than March 31, 1996. No liability is assumed for printing errors, lost, late or misdirected entries. Odds of winning are determined by the number of eligible entries distributed and received. Prizewinners will be determined no later than June 30, 1996.

Sweepstakes open to residents of the U.S. (except Puerto Rico), Canada, Europe and Taiwan who are 18 years of age or older. All applicable laws and regulations apply. Sweepstakes offer void wherever prohibited by law. Values of all prizes are in U.S. currency. This sweepstakes is presented by Torstar Corp., its subsidiaries and affiliates, in conjunction with book, merchandise and/or product offerings. For a copy of the Official Rules send a self-addressed, stamped envelope (WA residents need not affix return postage) to: MILLION DOLLAR SWEEPSTAKES (III) Rules, P.O. Box 4573, Blair, NE 68009, USA.

EXTRA BONUS PRIZE DRAWING

No purchase necessary. The Extra Bonus Prize will be awarded in a random drawing to be conducted no later than 5/30/96 from among all entries received. To qualify, entries must be received by 3/31/96 and comply with published directions. Drawing open to residents of the U.S. (except Puerto Rico), Canada, Europe and Taiwan who are 18 years of age or older. All applicable laws and regulations apply; offer void wherever prohibited by law. Odds of winning are dependent upon number of eligibile entries received. Prize is valued in U.S. currency. The offer is presented by Torstar Corp., its subsidiaries and affiliates in conjunction with book, merchandise and/or product offering. For a copy of the Official Rules governing this sweepstakes, send a self-addressed, stamped envelope (WA residents need not affix return postage) to: Extra Bonus Prize Drawing Rules, P.O. Box 4590, Blair, NE 68009, USA.

SWP-S594

IT's our 1000th SILHOUETTE ROMANCE, AND WE'RE CELEBRATING!

JOIN US FOR A SPECIAL COLLECTION OF LOVE STORIES
BY AUTHORS YOU'VE LOVED FOR YEARS, AND
NEW FAVORITES YOU'VE JUST DISCOVERED.
JOIN THE CELEBRATION...

April
REGAN'S PRIDE by Diana Palmer
MARRY ME AGAIN by Suzanne Carey

May
THE BEST IS YET TO BE by Tracy Sinclair
CAUTION: BABY AHEAD by Marie Ferrarella

June
THE BACHELOR PRINCE by Debbie Macomber
A ROGUE'S HEART by Laurie Paige

July
IMPROMPTU BRIDE by Annette Broadrick
THE FORGOTTEN HUSBAND by Elizabeth August

SILHOUETTE ROMANCE...VIBRANT, FUN AND EMOTIONALLY
RICH! TAKE ANOTHER LOOK AT US! AND AS PART OF THE
CELEBRATION, READERS CAN RECEIVE A FREE GIFT!

YOU'LL FALL IN LOVE ALL OVER
AGAIN WITH
SILHOUETTE ROMANCE!

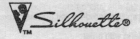

CEL1000

SILHOUETTE® Desire®

**Coming in May
from Silhouette Desire**

When an

Irresistible!

**man meets an unattainable woman...
sparks fly!**

**Look for these exciting men in books
created by some of the top authors in
contemporary romance:**

#853	LUCY AND THE STONE by Dixie Browning (Man of the Month)
#854	PERSISTENT LADY by Jackie Merritt
#855	BOTHERED by Jennifer Greene
#856	A LAWLESS MAN by Elizabeth Bevarly
#857	ONCE UPON A FULL MOON by Helen R. Myers
#858	WISH UPON A STARR by Nancy Martin

Don't miss them—only from Silhouette Desire!

CAN YOU STAND THE HEAT?

Silhouette ™

SUMMER Sizzlers '94

You're in for a serious heat wave with Silhouette's latest selection of sizzling summer reading. This sensuous collection of three short stories provides the perfect vacation escape! And what better authors to relax with than

ANNETTE BROADRICK
JACKIE MERRITT
JUSTINE DAVIS

And that's not all....

With the purchase of *Silhouette Summer Sizzlers '94*, you can send in for a FREE Summer Sizzlers beach bag!

SUMMER JUST GOT HOTTER— WITH SILHOUETTE BOOKS!